# RULER
# OF THE
# RANGE

# RULER
## of the
# RANGE

# Peter
# Dawson

**Thorndike Press • Chivers Press**
**Thorndike, Maine USA  Bath, England**

This Large Print edition is published by Thorndike Press, USA and by Chivers Press, England.

Published in 1997 in the U.S. by arrangement with Golden West Literary Agency.

Published in 1997 in the U.K. by arrangement with Golden West Literary Agency.

U.S. Hardcover   0-7862-1077-X   (Western Series Edition)
U.K. Hardcover   0-7540-3018-0   (Chivers Large Print)
U.K. Softcover   0-7540-3019-9   (Camden Large Print)

This book appeared serially in the *Saturday Evening Post*, issues of October 17 through December 1, 1951.

Thorndike Large Print ® Western Series.

The text of this Large Print edition is unabridged.
Other aspects of the book may vary from the original edition.

Set in 16 pt. Plantin by Rick Gundberg.

Printed in the United States on permanent paper.

**British Library Cataloguing in Publication Data available**

**Library of Congress Cataloging in Publication Data**

Dawson, Peter, 1907–
    Ruler of the range / Peter Dawson.
     p.  cm.
    ISBN 0-7862-1077-X (lg. print : hc)
    1. Large type books.  I. Title.
    [PS3507.A848R79   1997]
    813'.54—dc21                      97-330

# Cast of Characters

**JEFF KINDRED** meant to give up his spread in only one case — when he was dead.

**NOAH HORN,** Jeff's partner, would straighten out when the chips were down, Jeff knew.

**FRANK SORRELL,** owner of the Wineglass, offered Jeff money and then lead.

**HUGH CODRICK,** smooth and urbane, was playing a game Jeff couldn't fathom.

**BEN OLDS,** narrow-faced foreman for Sorrell, would be glad to dry-gulch Jeff.

**CATHERINE HORN,** Jeff's third partner, would rather sell than start a range war.

# ONE

This was the fifth day of the storm. The land was sodden, drowning. A twelve-car sheep train that had pulled out of the southward hills at dawn took until three o'clock that afternoon covering the sixty-four miles to Cottonwood, having to slow to a crawl each time the rails bridged one of the innumerable washes overflowing with the roiling runoff. And it was cold even for late September, the steady drizzle now and then giving way to a flurry of mushy snow that greyed the sage-mottled flats.

Jeff Kindred, dozing on one of the seats in the cupola of the freight's caboose, wakened as the car lurched to a stop alongside the mired cattle pens at Cottonwood's out-skirts. For some moments he sat drowsily eyeing the hazy smother of blue woodsmoke lying back along the softening grade, aware only of the chill that had made its way into this drafty, glass-enclosed cubicle. Then, though he tried to force his thoughts to remain idle, the worry and that alien de-pression began stirring in him once more.

He shortly lifted his scuffed boots from the cushion opposite, straightened his long frame from its slouch, and stretched to ease the cramp from the muscles of his heavy shoulders, aware of voices coming from the car below. Some seconds later steps sounded out of the narrow aisle and he looked down to see Fred Ordway, the shipper, come to the foot of the ladder and glance up at him.

"Need some air. Want to come along outside?"

"Not this time," Kindred answered, and watched Ordway go on toward the car's rear.

Kindred was thinking then, as he had several times before, of the incongruity of Fred Ordway being a sheepman. Young, likeable, Ordway had taken the constant baiting of the brakeman and conductor good-humoredly throughout the day, betraying none of the rancor their caustic remarks must have aroused in him. He had won some of their money, and a little of Kindred's, at the game of draw poker that had gone on since midmorning. His friendliness, his easy laugh, had made the day more bearable for Kindred.

The faint ring of the sheepman's boots against the car's platform steps outside brought Kindred's glance around to the nearby window now, and he looked down to see Ordway saunter into sight to join the brakeman, who stood with shoulders hunched, the bale of a lighted lantern held in the crook of an elbow. The two began talking, their breathing laying a misty vapor before their faces, the brakie's expression one of plain disgruntlement at having to be out in the weather, Fred Ordway's holding its familiar quality of cheerfulness.

Presently Kindred reached to the pocket of his rough wool coat and took out a pipe and a buckskin pouch of tobacco. When his glance went below again, the pipe packed, it was to see both men below staring at something up along the line of the cars. Curious as to what had taken their attention, he turned to peer out of the cupola's forward-facing window.

A man wearing a long buffalo coat and a wide grey hat was plodding this way along the cinder path flanking the cars. At first disbelief was strong in Kindred as he thought he recognized the figure. Then, knowing he couldn't be mistaken, irritation stirred in him and he asked himself, *What the devil can he be doing across here?*

His mood was larded with a sober dislike, almost a resentment, as he watched the man approach the two below, speak briefly to them, then disappear in the direction of the caboose steps. In another moment he was hearing the door slam, and steps approaching along the aisle below.

Then the man down there must have noticed Kindred's legs hanging in the well of the cupola. For he glanced up, and a surprise that wasn't quite convincing crossed his slender, blond-moustached face.

"Well, I'm damned! Look who's here," he breathed, smiling broadly. "A fine balmy day, eh, Jeff?"

"You can have it, Codrick."

The other laughed softly, ignoring the faint edge of unfriendliness in Kindred's drawl. He unbuckled the heavy coat, looked around for a place to hang it. Finding none, he laid it on the floor in front of a pair of lockers. His slight, medium-tall frame was clad in an expensive grey suit, and now he reached down to brush off the cuffs of his trousers, afterward pulling himself up to take the seat opposite Kindred in the cupola.

"Had to come across here yesterday and get a deposition for that toll road case of Mr. Sorrell's," he announced. "This is the first train they've run north all day. Storm's bogged the line down."

Kindred nodded. "Didn't know there

10

could be this much rain," he said, speaking merely to be saying something.

"Cathy mentioned you'd wired Noah you were due back today." The words startled Kindred, for he had this moment been thinking of Catherine Horn and her brother, Noah, his two ranch partners. And there was a faint, unreasonable resentment stirring in him as the man added, "It occurred to me you just might be aboard."

Kindred wasn't welcoming the prospect of having to ride on home, to Ledge, in the company of this Hugh Codrick. For the man's smooth manner, the visible signs of affluence about him, seemed to accent all the troubles and concern that had been plaguing Kindred these past ten days. And it cost him a real effort to speak civilly now, to say, "We'll be lucky to make it across the pass before dark."

"You will. I go only as far as Gap. More toll road business. Guess I'll hire a rig and drive across tonight." There was a definite aloofness in the way Codrick eyed Kindred then to say off handedly, "Hear you've been away trying for a loan."

A slow anger stirred in Kindred at this bland voicing of his troubles, though he understood that the anger was unreasonable and checked an acid retort, instead nodding matter-of-factly, saying nothing.

"Have any luck?" Codrick queried.

"Not any."

The lawyer shook his head, sighing. "Don't know how you're to hold on, Jeff."

"We will," Kindred said tonelessly.

Codrick's look turned speculative and he stared at Kindred a long moment, at length saying, "Something's come up since you left. Another offer on your place."

"Another? You mean another of Frank Sorrell's?"

"No. This is from a new man. He'll go a cool thousand higher than Mr. Sorrell."

"On Noah's and Catherine's share?"

"No. He'd want all of Ladder. Their half and yours."

"Then it's no go," Kindred stated flatly. "You ought to know by now I'm hanging onto my half."

The engine's whistle shrilled from up ahead just then and both men sat wordless as the bang of slack couplings traveled the length of the train. Codrick reached inside his coat as the car jerked into motion, taking out two cigars and offering one. Kindred lifted the pipe he had forgotten to light and the lawyer pocketed one cigar, afterward biting the end from the other, then scratching a match across the varnished wood and offering Kindred a light.

Kindred was drawing on the pipe as the door below slammed and the brakie and Ordway came along the aisle. The trainman looked up as he passed, saying, "Let's get the game goin' again and gang up on this herder."

"Be along later," Kindred told him, and he went on.

In another moment Codrick was staring through the smoke of his cigar to say, "Look, Jeff. No one could have known you were buying into a bad luck outfit year before last when you put your money into Ladder. But that's exactly what it's been for you. Bad luck. Get out from under while you can, before it's too late."

"Why should I?" Kindred countered. "If we have one good year, just one, we're in the clear."

There was a coolness, a smugness to the smile that patterned the lawyer's handsome face then. "If," he said, accenting that one word. "There are too many ifs. If that blizzard last spring had dumped those drifts beyond either of the Elk creek ridges you wouldn't have had those carcasses piled higher than your fence. If Noah hadn't thrown his first big spree trying to forget Ladder's winter kill he wouldn't have the makings of a souse now. If —"

"Noah'll straighten out," Kindred cut in.

"Now will he?" the lawyer asked blandly, continuing, "maybe I should've told you this right off. Noah's been gone for a solid week."

Kindred was struck by a strong shock and alarm. "Drunk?"

Codrick shrugged. "Who knows? But he's away somewhere. Without having told anyone he was going. He didn't show up to work your end of the gather. No one's seen him since."

Kindred sat weighing the implications to the lawyer's words, a slow dread settling through him. "Does Catherine know?"

"She must. Must be half out of her mind with worry."

Codrick eyed Kindred half-amusedly now, saying, "So add it all up, but there it is. Back when you made your deal with Noah and Cathy you couldn't have known how he'd turn out. He was as fine a person as his sister, and we both know there's no one finer than Cathy. I don't mind telling you I intend marrying her one day if she'll have me."

He saw Kindred about to interrupt and lifted a hand. "But that's neither here nor there, Jeff. What you've got to understand is that drinking is in Noah Horn's blood.

Old man Horn was a drinker, which is the reason the outfit needed money when he died. Furthermore, Noah hasn't the guts his sister has. If he did, would he lay down on you like this, let you do two-thirds of the work? No. He'd be working his hands raw. Like Cathy's working, running that bake store in town, trying to help keep up Ladder's interest payments."

The bleak realization of the truth of what the lawyer was saying struck home to Kindred. Yet his loyalty and affection for his partner made him say doggedly, "He was off the bottle for five whole weeks. So let him have his fling now. When he shows up he'll straighten out again."

"He may, you mean," Codrick said. "But there's another of your ifs. *If* he straightens up and works you may pull through."

The man's smugness grated so harshly against Kindred's patience that he let himself drawl caustically, "And if we didn't have a neighbor wanting to crowd us out we'd have a chance with the bank."

The lawyer nodded. "That may be. I'll admit Wineglass has made it harder for you. Admit it even if I do Mr. Sorrell's law work."

"Mister!" Kindred flared. "He can't be just plain Sorrell, like you're plain Codrick

15

and I'm Kindred. No, he's so damned high and mighty people're afraid to call him anything but Mr. Sorrell. Why?"

"One of those things. Some men command that kind of respect."

"Command it, hell! He buys it," Kindred raged quietly. "He's got Wineglass, he's the same as got the bank. He's got a feed mill and a lumber camp. Now you're helping him get a toll road."

"Don't take it out on me, Jeff. I only work for him."

The anger was bright in Kindred's dark eyes now as he finally let himself openly show his dislike for this man. "It was your idea, wasn't it, advising him he could kick those folks off their land for back taxes? Now we'll all have to pay him to travel a road people have used since this country was opened up."

He took in the way the lawyer's face lost color, the momentary ash of anger in the other's eyes. And suddenly wanting to put an end to this pointless argument, he reached out to the guard-rail and swung down into the aisle, afterward looking up to say, "Well, one thing he doesn't have is Ladder. He won't get it directly, and he won't get it by having someone else buy it for him."

"This man who's made the offer isn't buying for Sorrell," Codrick stated brittlely. "You have my word on that."

"Who is this man?"

The lawyer shook his head. "He's asked not to be named."

"Why has he?"

"Just a whim probably. But I have to respect a client's confidence if he asks it."

"Well, tell your client my share's not for sale." Remembering something then, he was regretting having shown so much of his anger. And his tone was quite gentle as he asked, "By the way, how's your father?"

"No better. It could happen any day, or he could drag on a while longer."

"He's still up and around?"

"Most of the time. Won't give in till they get another man to look after his patients."

"A shame," Kindred said gravely. "We all hate to see it happening. Say hello to him for me."

"I will." Codrick stared obliquely down into the shadows, asking, "This is your last word? You wouldn't want me to go after my man to boost his price?"

"No. Ladder's what I want. I'll hang on."

"You may be hauling a double load, don't forget."

"Then I'll haul it." And Kindred turned away.

Lightning had been playing fitfully across the foothills above Gap ever since the brief stop there to let Hugh Codrick leave the train. In the hour and forty minutes since, there had been a constant screeching of the wheels against the bends making the climb toward Eagle Pass. That sound, along with the intermittent slashing of the rain against the cupola windows, had pulled at the nerves of the four men sitting at the make-shift table. It was dark now, though the hour was barely past five.

The brakie, at the finish of one hand, cocked his head and frowned, listening. And as the cards were being dealt again he climbed around the conductor along the padded bench and disappeared up the steps into the cupola.

Returning shortly, he muttered, "Turns a man's hair grey to think of how soft this grade must be."

"Not your hair, Sam," came Fred Ordway's dry rejoinder.

"Anyway, we're over the hump. Just," the trainman said, pointedly ignoring this reference to his baldness.

The words had their effect upon Jeff Kindred as he realized that the train must be coming down onto Ladder range. He held two pair on that deal, a good hand, yet he nonetheless threw in his cards and eased back against the cushions, cocking his big frame around so as to look out the window behind him.

It was almost half a minute before lightning flickered to show him a familiar vista. The freight was crawling around the edge of Mirror Lake, and a nostalgia rose in him as he glimpsed the break in the fringe of spruce across the water that was the head of the trail climbing around Ladder's high meadow. And suddenly he was feeling better than he had in days, in weeks, the sense of being home again warming his chilled thoughts. This was where he belonged. Here was where he had put his roots down. Nothing, not even debt and a partner he couldn't count on, was going to take Ladder from him.

A series of bright purple flashes, and sharp crackling reports like the thunder of half a hundred heavy rifles, cut across his ruminations that instant. The burst of light outside nearly blinded him, and he could see the mile-wide stretch of meadow as brightly lit as by day.

Then, as the last hard echoes of the thunder rolled out of hearing into the downward distance, he was hearing Ordway say, "That ought to bust something loose. Damn, won't it ever let —"

A low, vibrating rumble cut across the sheepman's words, making him pause in mid-sentence. A second later came three sharp, jerky wails of the locomotive's whistle.

The whistle's shriek was all at once cut off, and the conductor lunged from the bench across from Kindred in quick panic as the rumble mounted quickly to a gathering roar. "A slide!" the trainman bellowed, his voice hoarse with terror.

Suddenly, with that scant warning, the caboose slammed to such a vicious stop that Jeff Kindred was hurled sideways along the bench and hard against the car's end wall. The desk-lid they had been using as their table came cartwheeling after him, Ordway's off-balance weight driving after it. And Kindred barely managed to twist to one side and get to his feet as the wood grazed his thigh and banged against the wall.

That instant the shaded bracket lamp swung hard against the roof, shattered, and threw the car into pitch blackness except for the feeble flicker of a small flame. The brakie shouted stridently, "Run for it!" as the caboose tilted sharply, then jolted upright again.

A tongue of flame all at once licked upward from the floor, letting Kindred see the two trainmen lunging out the door at the car's far end. Ordway lay close by, struggling to get his legs from under the desk-lid, and Kindred reached down and hauled the man to his feet, saying, "Let's move!" a measure of the panic that had been in the two others clawing at him now.

They made the back platform, Ordway first, Kindred feeling a sense of relief as he breathed fresh air rather than the reek of coal oil inside the car. He vaulted the rail close on the heels of the sheepman, coming erect after his knees had buckled, his panic gone. He called, "Hold it!" for now he could hear nothing but an awesome, absolute silence.

Ordway's voice came from close to his left. "Good Lord! What must've happened to the boys up front?"

Kindred had been thinking of the same thing and now said quickly, "We'll go see. What happened to the others?"

"Sam said to run for it. Guess they did." Ordway raised his voice to a shout. "Sam!"

Sight of a flickering light through the caboose door carried Kindred on up the steps. He was pulling off his coat the instant after pushing the door open, and he was vaguely aware of a bawling, a frantic bleating close beyond the windows as he beat at the flames spreading across the puddled boards. Then Ordway was there, throwing a slicker over the fiercest blaze. In a few more seconds the fire was out, the car dark and silent once more.

An urgency was driving Kindred now as he snapped, "We'll need axes and lanterns. Where would they be?"

"Right here." Ordway moved close beside him. The next moment the man struck a match and went to his knees before a locker at the foot of the nearest bench.

He lifted out a pair of axes and a heavy crow bar as Kindred, once again aware of the clamor of the sheep, drawled, "Doesn't sound too good for you out there, Fred."

"Brother, I'm just plain glad to be alive."

"But you've got something besides your skin to lose in this."

"The hell with that right now. Let's go."

They lit lanterns, pulled on their slickers and, carrying the tools, went out into the rainy night. A huddle of grey shapes moved away from them as they ran along the line of the cars, Kindred once nearly falling as he collided with a frightened ewe.

The eighth car ahead of the caboose was tilted, leaning precariously over the grade's edge. From inside it came a rattle of hooves and a bawling that rose over that of the animals running loose.

"We'll take the inside from here on," Kindred said, all at once remembering that along this stretch the grade hung above a gorge running from the foot of the meadow to form the headwaters of Elk Creek. And now as he pictured the hundred-foot drop to the bottom of the cut he was more afraid than ever for the lives of the men in the locomotive.

They found the next two cars lying on their sides, their roofs twisted open. They came upon a third overturned car. It was beyond this that the pale wash of their lanterns picked out a down-slanting grey shadow that engulfed the front half of the next car.

"Buried!" Ordway breathed, his voice barely audible as he eyed the enormity of the slide. "What a god-awful way to die!"

Kindred was stubbornly refusing to believe what his eyes told him. He climbed the nearby sky-slanted truck onto the car's side, lifting the lantern high as he could, trying to see over the embankment's edge. But the drop-off was too steep to be caught by the light. Behind the sibilant hissing of the rain and the bleating of the sheep he imagined he could catch the faint, low roar of the creek sounding from far below.

When Ordway stood beside him, he said, "A man might be able to cross it," and started up along the shifting rubble. He had taken but four cautious steps when the talus gave way under him and he fell sprawling. He was still sliding when Ordway's hold on his slicker dragged him to the sound footing of the car's side.

"Two's enough," the sheepman said in a quavering tone. "Don't scare me that way again."

Kindred stood letting his breathing shallow after those seconds of hard exertion. He was trying to glimpse something along the face of the slide, steam vapor or smoke, to tell him that the engine lay buried here and hadn't been swept off into the gorge's depths.

Finally, neither seeing nor hearing a thing to help him decide, he looked around at Ordway. "Well, do we just stand here?"

There was an angry edge to his voice, and the sheepman answered in much the same tone, "Name something better to do."

Kindred sighed in honest bafflement, trying to hold onto his stubborn belief that there must still be some chance that the two men were alive. For a long moment he stared outward over the slide, and during that interval there came a faint shout from back along the grade in the direction of the caboose.

"They're a big help," Ordway said listlessly.

Kindred paid the words little attention as he gazed down at the door of the car. "Yellow," he said, noticing the paint peeling from the planks. "It was the only yellow one in the lot. First one behind the engine."

When he hesitated, Ordway drawled, "Meanin' what, friend?"

"We could break into this car and tunnel through from the front end to the tender. If it's there."

"If."

Kindred gave the sheepman a solemn look, then nodded to the blackness beyond. "You think they're down below?"

"Don't know what to think."

"Neither do I. Feel like giving the other a try?"

"It'd maybe take us the whole night. Hell, this stuff's like sand. A man couldn't dig through it."

Kindred was thinking of something else, and shortly drawled, "There's an old lady lives a mile or so below in a mine shack. She works the mine, leases it from me and my partners. Her name's Grace Hill. Sam could hoof it down there and borrow a horse from her, go to town for help. You and I could try our luck at using some planks to shore in a hole and dig through."

"So we could." The sheepman gave Kindred a look that was speculative, faintly amused. "Y' know, you're more bullheaded than me even. Where'd you learn it?"

"Learn what?"

"Never to give up." Ordway waited for a reply. Getting none, he at length turned away, muttering, "Let's get at it."

Hugh Codrick finished his business in Gap at about the time Kindred and Ordway began chopping their way through the front end of the boxcar, after Kindred had told the brakeman how to find the mine where he was to ask old Grace Hill the loan of a horse.

Codrick had had some dealings with a store owner in Gap, and it took him only a few more minutes to borrow a buggy and team from the man and start out along the pass road. And it was some twenty minutes after leaving Gap that the lamps of the buggy picked out a pair of weed-grown ruts leaving the main road and cutting back through a stand of aspen. Codrick reined the team along this abandoned track, hurrying now, wanting to be out of sight of the main road as quickly as possible.

He had gone on perhaps a hundred yards when suddenly a thick-barreled dun horse carrying a big man in the saddle stepped from behind a clump of oak brush close ahead.

Though he had halfway been expecting an encounter of this nature, the lawyer was nevertheless startled enough to speak with an edge to his tone as he drew alongside the rider. "Well, how did it go?"

"Passable."

The speaker was a man of massive proportions, his slicker failing to hide the outline of heavy-muscled, sloping shoulders and thick upper body. Black beard stubble darkened his blocky face. His expression was almost menacing as he drawled, "You took your time. Noon, you said it was to be."

"Couldn't help that. I caught the first train north."

"I been freezin' off and on here for six hours."

Codrick checked an imperious retort, his better judgment telling him he would only be hurting himself if he spoke his mind. "Sorry, Reno. There was nothing I could do about it. Anything go wrong?"

"Not a thing. We heard the train come

through and figured you'd be along. So my partner's down there now pourin' the coffee into him."

"Does Horn know where he is?"

"Didn't when I left." The big man spoke patiently, though now as he shivered and lifted his wet hands to blow on them it was quite obvious he would have no regrets when this interchange was over.

Noticing that, Codrick nevertheless said, "We'd better go over it once more before you take me in. How was he on the way across from Frenchy's last night?"

"Drunk. Didn't have to mix the stuff from the bottle you gave me but twice when he sobered some. It put him to sleep right away both times. What's in the bottle?"

"It's called chloral hydrate."

"Get it from your old man?"

Codrick nodded in irritation, nervously changing the subject by saying, "Now about what you two're to do. I'd like —"

"We got it down pat. All but the money."

"It's here." Codrick reached inside his coat, asking as he drew out a bulging bill fold, "What about Grace Hill?"

"What about her? I been on this other for six days now."

"Get back there to the mine soon as you can," the lawyer said. "Tonight. Only be careful how you go in. She's old and probably doesn't sleep much. She might be working at night. It would be bad if she spotted your light."

"We take our chances on that, don't we?" Reno countered. "Damned if I climb those slippery ladders in there without no lantern."

"Just be careful is all."

Codrick was taking several banknotes from his wallet as the big man unexpectedly drawled, "This begins to add up, don't it?"

The lawyer's head lifted sharply. "What does?"

"Playin' the soft spots, drunks and old women."

Codrick stiffened, waiting. Then, when Reno didn't go on, he asked coldly, "What're you trying to say?"

Reno shrugged. "Nothin'. But that mine the old girl leases is on Ladder range. And Horn and his sister own half Ladder."

"So?"

"So it looks to me like you might be tryin' to make a grab."

The lamplight showed the slow, broad smile that had come to the big man's face. Furious, Codrick said in a grating voice, "Any time you want to call it quits and stop collecting your ten dollars a day, say the word, Reno."

The other's expression quickly took on a contriteness. "Now who said I wanted to call it quits?"

"Then forget the guesses," Codrick snapped. "Forget everything but what I ask you to do."

"Suits me," the big man agreed meekly.

Codrick handed the money across now. Reno counted the bills, then reached under his slicker to pocket them, saying, "One thing I don't get is what makes you so sure Horn won't keep this money after I've handed it to him."

"He won't. I know he won't."

"But suppose he does?"

"Then you'll get more," Codrick answered gruffly. "Now let's get on with this." And he lifted the reins.

The other made no move to put his horse in motion, drawling, "You better hoof it from here. The shack's just ahead."

Grudgingly, Codrick laid aside the laprobe the buggy's owner had loaned him. He turned up the collar of the coat before stepping aground. And Reno, taking the nearest animal's rein, wound it about the branch of a bush, afterward saying, "Better hang onto me. It's darker'n the bottom of a well."

Codrick took a hold on the big man's

30

slicker and they started on. Shortly the lawyer was seeing lamplight glowing from a window through the trees ahead, and in several more seconds he could make out the faint outline of a cabin.

Reno shortly drew rein, saying in a low voice, "There's a shed against the back wall. Get in there and you can hear everything. I'll give you a couple minutes to get set."

"Remember, Horn's not to ride back with you," Codrick said. He was hesitating, and a moment later asked, "What about this other man? You haven't told him about me?"

"Only that someone'll be listenin' when we lay down the chips to Horn. He's nothin' but a brush jumper on his way through, doin' his best to stay out of sight. The twenty's all he's after."

Satisfied, the lawyer turned away. "See me tomorrow night in town then. Same place. Say six-thirty."

He got no reply, had expected none, and he started off through the trees thinking chiefly of hurrying, of cutting short the time he was to be exposed to the weather, for he was a fastidious man little used to such hardship and discomfort as this.

Half a minute later he was walking in on a shed at the rear of the small cabin. He approached it slowly, cautiously, for the first time today really aware of the weight of the .44 Navy Colt he had dropped in the deep pocket of the coat yesterday before leaving home. His hand was in the pocket feeling the weapon's reassuring weight as he edged in through the shed's door.

He was no sooner inside than he was seeing a line of feeble lamplight glowing between two logs at the level of his waist. He crouched there in the blackness to stare through the slit, his pulse at once quickening at what he saw inside the cabin.

The first thing that met his glance was Noah Horn's shape sprawled on the dirt floor opposite, less than a dozen feet away. The man's clothes were grimy with half-dried mud, his dark head was pillowed on a ragged blanket, his eyes were closed.

To this side of that outstretched figure, a lantern sat in the dirt close beside a puddle marking the spot where rain had soaked through the rotten roof. The lantern's chimney was sooted, its light struggling against the darkness. A rusty stove filled the corner to Codrick's right, smoke pluming lazily from a hole in its chimney.

All at once a seedy, narrow-faced man he had never seen before moved into his line of vision, stepping slowly across to look down at Noah. Then shortly a sound from in front of the cabin made the man turn and step out of sight again. In several more seconds Codrick was hearing the squeal of hinges and the sound of Reno's deep voice saying something that was unintelligible.

Both men moved into sight then, Reno in the process of shrugging out of the slicker. The big man looked across at Noah, then around at his companion. Codrick plainly saw him close an eye in a slow wink before he stepped over and reached down to shake Noah's shoulder, saying, "On your feet, partner. Our man's been here with the money."

Noah Horn's head lifted feebly from the blanket. He blinked his eyes. Then he was saying in a thick voice, "How . . . where are we?"

"All right," Reno sighed in a tone of tried patience, "I'll tell it once more. Only you got to listen this time." Pausing briefly, he asked, "Remember the game up at Frenchy Duval's last night?"

"Las' night? Seems . . . seems like a long time ago." Noah pushed up onto an elbow, running a hand across his face before he looked up to mumble, "Wh . . . what about th' game?"

"You and me, Frenchy and this here gent was playin'."

Noah stared sleepily at the other man, slowly nodding, and Reno went on, "You lost to me to the tune of fifty dollars. Remember?"

"I remem . . . I was losing, sure. But where're we now?"

"We're the other side of the hills, fella." Reno spoke gently. "When the game broke up we had some drinks. Remember?" At Noah's second nod, he went on, "Then's when I put you the notion of takin' this ride. Hell, you owed me. You had to pay up some way."

Codrick was watching Noah intently and saw the strong bewilderment that came to that slender face so strikingly like Cathy's. And now Noah drawled in a voice heavy with despair, "I don't . . . nothing comes back, Reno. Nothing after the drinks."

The big man lifted hands outward from his sides in a helpless gesture. "I told you how I'd spotted this bunch of young stuff it wouldn't be hard to push across here, what with the rain and all. Said I'd need help, said we'd forget the fifty if you come along. There was a bird across here who'd take 'em off our hands, I told you."

Over a slight pause, he continued, "You and me and Dooley here spent most of last night wadin' them animals up Dead Horse cut and across through all this muck. Then today you slept it off while him and me rode down a ways and scouted out my friend. He's already paid me off and sent his crew on with the critters. So here you are."

He drew the roll of money from his pocket now, thumbing several bills from it, drawling, "And ten makes thirty, and two fives comes to forty." He offered the money, adding, "Never say I didn't treat you square, Horn. Your share comes to ninety dollars. Less the fifty you owed me leaves forty. Here, take it."

Noah stared at the bills. "Where . . . whose cattle were they?" he asked in an alarmed and surprisingly steady voice.

"Wineglass's. Frank Sorrell's. Who else's?" Reno's faintly amused glance clung warily to him, watching the way he took this. Then abruptly he was asking, "You ready to ride for home?"

Noah shook his head savagely. "That's not for me."

"Hell it ain't. You earned it."

All at once Noah reached up and struck Reno's hand, hit it so hard that the bills fluttered to the dirt. Then he was saying in a grating voice, "Take your money and clear out. Take it!"

Reno had moved backward a step, his

heavy frame going tense as though he was halfway looking for real trouble. "Now hold on, partner," he said in a soothing way. "Damned if I got any combin' over coming from you."

The change that came over Noah that moment was as abrupt as the one of a moment ago. He let his spare body sink to the floor once more, murmuring dismally and in a voice that was almost a whisper, "So now I'm a rustler too."

"Y' got a few things to learn before you're a good one." Reno reached down and picked up the money, brandishing it as he drawled, "Your last chance. Take this or it's mine."

"It's yours."

Noah didn't even look up. Reno shrugged and turned away, stepping on out of Codrick's line of vision. In another moment he reappeared, one of his fingers hooked in the handle of an earthenware jug.

He set the jug on the floor within Noah's reach, saying dryly, "Might need some hair of the dog before you make it home, Horn. You'll find your nag tied out front. Your hull's there behind the stove." Hesitating, staring down at Noah, he shortly asked, "Sure you ain't comin' with us?"

Noah only shook his head. So, glancing

around at the other man, smiling briefly, Reno drawled, "Then we're on our way." He pulled his slicker on and with a nod at Dooley led the way to the door.

At the slam of the door, Noah's head lifted briefly from the blanket. Never had Codrick seen the man's face so old-looking, its expression so bitter and remorseful.

Codrick had seen and heard all that was necessary. Nothing that had taken place these last two minutes had even faintly surprised him, except for Reno having been so sure of himself. He had planned this carefully. There had never been the slightest doubt in him as to what the outcome would be. And now nothing but a sadistic curiosity was keeping him here.

For nearly five minutes Noah lay there without moving. But suddenly, just as the lawyer came to his feet and was on the point of edging away from the wall, he pushed up to a sitting position. He stared at the jug, eyeing it with a cold anger brightening the look in his eyes. All at once he reached out and lifted the jug. Drawing back his arm, he threw it viciously at the stove.

The jug shattered with a crash that made Codrick start. He saw Noah slump face down against the blanket once more. Then he could hear Noah's smothered sobbing against the murmur of the rain.

Only then did Hugh Codrick soundlessly stalk from the shed. There was a glowing satisfaction in him as he hurried off into the trees. On his walk back to the buggy he once thought of Cathy but quickly put her from mind as he looked back upon what he had seen and heard in the cabin. It was something that would make his long drive home to Ledge less wearisome, for he had much to think about.

That afternoon, at about the time the sheep train was pulling out of Cottonwood, a man had ridden in to Ledge from the gather camp ten miles north and gone straight to Catherine Horn's bakery. He had brought Cathy the news that she could be the means of staving off a major disaster. With the weather so foul and wood so wet, the cook was having all he could do to feed the crew beans, stew and coffee, let alone keep his ovens going for the baking of breads and pies. The men were complaining, the cook was threatening to quit. Would Cathy bake up a big batch of bread and pies and have them ready to be picked up by someone from the camp at seven tomorrow morning?

Cathy had agreed. And now, the supper

dishes done, she and Maud Wilson, her helper, were getting the bread ready for the oven, Cathy working at the big table in the back room of the shop mechanically buttering a row of pans.

She was a tall, slender girl with sandy red hair and eyes of so dark a brown that in this lamplight they appeared to be black. The expression on her delicate yet strong-featured face was preoccupied as she thought of Noah in much the same way as she had thought of him this afternoon, this morning, yesterday and the day before, ever since first learning that he hadn't shown up to work Ladder's share in the rounding up of the shipping herd.

The only explanation she could give her brother's strange absence was that he must be drinking again in the way he had several times this past summer. Looking back over the months, she was remembering the day his appetite for alcohol had changed from an occasional hilarious release to become a sordid, unwanted habit.

The first time she had ever seen him really sodden under the influence of whiskey was the night early last spring after he and Jeff Kindred had ridden their lower north fence, the one separating their range from Wineglass's, to count upward of a hundred dead

Ladder-branded cattle piled in windrows along the wire, buried by the drifts. He had come to her that night not only as a younger brother seeking his sister's solace but as her partner and Kindred's, to tell her that their firm hope of being able to free Ladder from debt this year was gone, wiped out by that vicious, late blizzard.

He had been heartsick, so beaten that he had never regained his carefreeness and his drive. Since then he had inwardly taken on a cynical maturity far beyond his twenty years. And although he had seemingly worked as hard as Kindred to make up Ladder's loss, Cathy knew that his hopes had never revived in the stubborn, unbeaten way their partner's had.

Now, thinking of Kindred and remembering that his telegram to Noah had said he would be returning to Ledge today, she was suddenly longing to see the man. Simply because Kindred had had little hope of being able to borrow the money that would take the load off their backs, she doubted that he would return with it. Yet she still wanted to see him, to talk to him and be bolstered by his calm, unruffled manner. He would be able to do something about Noah whereas she was tied down here, powerless.

Thinking this, it struck her as odd that

she had come to rely on him so heavily. For, except for now and then discussing the ranch's affairs with him, their relationship had been impersonal, almost casual. She scarcely knew him, or so it would seem. Yet she did know him well enough to be certain of his strength and his level-headedness. That was what mattered now.

She was all at once startled to hear Maud Wilson say, "Cathy, you ought to let me finish this. Go out for a walk and get your mind off things."

Cathy realized she had been standing before the table staring vacantly at the wall. And suddenly she did want to leave the store, to be alone with her thoughts. "Maybe I will. For just a few minutes," she said, and at Maud's nod she took off her apron and went on into the back room that served as her living quarters.

A minute later, coming onto the street wearing her wool coat and carrying an umbrella, she had decided that she would go to Hugh Codrick. Though there was no elation in her at the prospect of talking with him, she understood that he would help her in any way he could. And perhaps he would know of something she could do in trying to find out what had happened to Noah.

It was but a minute's walk down the street

to Doctor Codrick's house. She saw a light in the office window as she turned off the walk fronting the house, and on the way up the porch steps she saw the medico sitting in an easy chair in the window bay. She opened the door bearing its placard, *Please Enter Without Knocking*, and called as she stepped into the hallway, "Anyone home?"

The doctor's deep-tone voice answered from beyond the open office door. "Come in, Catherine. Come in."

The sight of him tiredly rising from the horsehair-upholstered chair in the window alcove made her say quickly, "Please don't get up," and hurry on around the long, leather-padded table at the room's center.

It had been two or three weeks since she had seen Hugh's father, and now she tried to hide the shock she felt at noticing the added gauntness of his face as she smiled down at him and accepted his hand.

His grip was firm, almost strong as he looked up at her to say seriously, "Catherine, sight of you most always makes me doubt an opinion of long standing."

"Opinion?" She was puzzled. "Which one, doctor?"

"The one I've always had that Mrs. Codrick was the most beautiful woman I should ever live to behold."

Her face flushing in pleasure, Cathy told him, "If you like, I'll let my hair go and wear an old dress when I come to see you."

The medico shook his head, a pallid smile easing the shadow of pain from his thin face. "No, you'd be denying me a genuine pleasure." Shifting in the chair, he went on, "You can't be here to see me professionally. I've never seen anyone looking finer."

"I was hoping to find Hugh at home."

"He isn't. Left yesterday to be gone till this afternoon. Over Gap way working on a case. I suppose the train's late." She must have shown her disappointment, for he at once said, "Something's worrying you. Can I help?"

She thought a great deal of William Codrick, and it occurred to her that he might be the one to talk to. Nevertheless, her pride rebelled, and she said quickly, "No, nothing's wrong." She turned to the door then, in her nervousness asking a pointless question, "Will you be wanting Maud tomorrow as usual, doctor?"

He nodded. "If you can spare her. She's a real help."

He was about to add something when abruptly the quick, heavy pound of boots crossing the porch made him peer out the window. "What's his hurry?" he asked gruffly.

They heard the door open, and that solid step came along the hallway. Then Pete Ballew, the blacksmith, appeared in the office doorway.

He had obviously been hurrying, for he was breathing hard as he burst out, "Doc, you're wanted. If you feel like comin', that is. Down at the station. There's been a sheep train wrecked up on the pass and they're makin' up a crew to haul help back. Mr. Sorrell says if you can come we'll see you keep warm and dry. He's sending a buggy for you."

"Someone hurt?" William Codrick was rising with difficulty from the chair.

"More likely dead," the blacksmith told him. "A slide either buried the engine or pushed it off into the cut below that meadow. This gent that brought the word down borrowed a horse from old Grace Hill up at the Difficult. She's probably up there by now, along with Jeff Kindred and the joker that owns the sheep. Jeff's workin' the hunch the engine stayed on the track. He's trying to tunnel through to it."

The medico was already on his way out the door. "Give me two minutes," he said as he went along the hallway.

Ballew smiled at Cathy, asking, "Been takin' any wooden nickels, Rusty?"

She didn't rise to his baiting reference to the color of her hair, something of long standing between them. Instead, thinking of Kindred, she asked, "Pete, could I go along? Would I be in the way?"

He was surprised and he sobered at once. Then, his smile returning, he said, "I should say not. Be glad to have you."

In two more hours, as Cathy gingerly picked her way down the dark slope beyond the slide toward the wrecked train, following the blacksmith who walked close ahead carrying a lantern, Kindred and Ordway were dragging the engineer's limp weight out of the locomotive's cab.

They breathed the foul air audibly, loudly, Ordway now and then coughing in a racking way as he pulled at the trainman's legs. Engine and tender lay on their sides, as did the car behind, this having made the work easier.

Two minutes ago the lantern had fallen and guttered out. Now no trace of light relieved the pitch blackness of this confined hole as Kindred grunted, "Here, let me get ahead of him and pull."

"What's wrong with me doin' it?"

The sheepman's reply was typical, Kindred was thinking. Ordway had worked like a man possessed these past four hours. His slight, wiry frame held a vast amount of energy, and he had toiled doggedly, not giving in to the disappointment of the tunnel from the boxcar's buried end having twice caved in.

Some forty minutes after they had started work, old Grace Hill had suddenly appeared in the car holding a strip of grimy canvas about her shoulders, clad as usual in her bib overalls and flat-heeled boots. She had shortly gone back to the caboose with the conductor to brew a pot of coffee, later making Kindred and Ordway pause in their work long enough to drink some of the steaming liquid.

It was while they had stood there alongside the aging recluse that Ordway had remarked bitterly, "We wouldn't be here now, those two wouldn't be buried under all that damned rock, if I'd played my hunch and waited to ship till the storm was over."

The old woman had said testily, in her typically blunt way, "What a fool thing to say! If this train hadn't been loaded with your sheep it would've been hauling some other man's cattle probably. Or grain, or hogs. So why the devil call it your fault? It was God that did it, Him and no one else."

Kindred couldn't recall ever before having experienced a disappointment as bitter as the one that came to him when finally, enough wood cleared from the tender to let them through, they had found the first man, the fireman, dead, crushed against the boiler by a mass of wood pinning him to the hot iron. He still lay back there where they had moved him so as to reach the engineer, who was still alive.

The sound of the unconscious trainman's labored breathing now roused an urgency in Kindred that made him push as best he could to help Ordway move the body's yielding weight. For a seemingly interminable interval they struggled awkwardly, inching toward the feeble light at the tunnel's mouth. Then at last a voice was saying, "Here, let me give you a hand," and in another moment the engineer's legs were dragged beyond Kindred's reach.

He lay exhausted, tiredly thankful to be breathing fresh air once more. He closed his eyes and gave in to the bone-deep weariness brought on by these hours of driving labor. Vaguely, hardly with any interest, he heard more voices sounding hollowly along the hole from the boxcar and realized apathetically that help must have arrived. Once he heard Grace Hill speaking, and a gratefulness stirred in him as he thought back on how the old woman had insisted on lugging the wood from the tunnel mouth as they cleared the tender.

Now, disinterestedly, he was able to distinguish what the nearer voices in the car were saying. He heard someone call, "Make way for the doc, boys," and thought it was Pete Ballew, the blacksmith, who had spoken.

Almost immediately another voice was gruffly asking, "You the sheepman?"

Kindred's alertness came alive at recognition of that voice. Then he was hearing Fred Ordway tiredly answer, "That's me."

"Has anyone told you that four bridges are washed out south of here? That the grade up north caved under the morning local?" There was an intolerant, scornful edge to the speaker's tone as he added, "The line's shut down. Will be for at least another month."

"What's that got to do with me, mister?"

"This is cattle country. You've thrown a pack of sheep among us. They're not wanted here."

"Not me," Ordway drawled patiently. "I didn't throw 'em here."

Jeff Kindred pushed onto hands and knees now and started crawling toward the faint light at the tunnel's mouth, hearing the other ask sharply, "What'll you do with these animals?"

"Anything you say."

Kindred pulled himself from the hole, staying on his knees to brush the grime from his coat and waist-overalls as Ordway was adding, "Hell, I don't like this any more'n you do."

Squinting into the glare of several lanterns, Kindred's glance took in the twelve or fifteen men grouped midway the length of the car. He knew some of them, men like Pete Ballew and the Ledge station agent. He saw narrow-faced Ben Olds, Frank Sorrell's ranch foreman, leaning indolently against the car's upended roof, another Wineglass crewman, Ralph Blake, alongside. The engineer lay stretched out in the near corner. Ailing Doctor Codrick knelt beside the man, stethoscope held to his chest.

Kindred felt a strong surprise at seeing Catherine Horn standing beside Grace Hill. Both women were pointedly watching the doctor in a way that indicated their uneasiness over the bickering they had been listening to. And now as Pete Ballew called, "Nice going, Jeff," the girl looked around, saw Kindred and gave him a strangely warm smile. He answered with a slow nod, though his awareness over these few seconds had been centered almost wholly upon a man who stood close by facing Ordway.

The man was Frank Sorrell. He was the one who had been speaking to the sheepman. With a glance down at Kindred now, he said tonelessly, "Glad you got to him in time, Kindred," his regard at once settling on the sheepman again.

Sorrell's square face, its jawline made squarer by a close-cropped and greying spade beard, took on a stony look. "I'd recommend penning your sheep and hauling feed," he said. "They're not to be brought any lower onto this range."

Over the next brief interval there was no sound in the car except for the unconscious man's loud breathing. Not one of the onlookers moved. Though most of them appeared uncomfortable, on edge, not a man spoke, and Kindred was angrily aware of the awed respect which these men held for Frank Sorrell as he came erect now.

The next moment Fred Ordway's quiet words were striking across the uneasy silence. "And who's to foot the bill for the feed?"

"You'll foot it."

"Feed for a month? How could I? All my stake's on the hoof. Every dollar of it."

"Credit can be arranged."

"How can it?"

"You can surrender bills of sale on your sheep."

The look of weary, baffled anger that crossed Ordway's face that moment made Kindred say, "Doesn't the railroad foot the bill, Sorrell? They took Ordway's shipment. It's up to them to deliver." He looked on past Sorrell to the station agent. "How about it, Kemp?"

The agent shrugged, "This storm's given us the devil of a lot of trouble. I doubt they'd pay him a dime."

Kindred met Sorrell's beetling stare directly once more, telling himself, *Let it ride. This isn't your worry, so why buy into it?* though the next moment he knew he would stand by Ordway regardless, stand by him because he liked and respected him, because the man didn't deserve this kicking around that might well ruin him.

Now Sorrell said in deceiving mildness, "No one invited this man to haul his sheep across cattle range. He could've gone south, which is where sheep belong. Now he's here, let him look out for himself."

Kindred felt the anger tightening in him and turned away, trying to think of some way of satisfying Sorrell without hurting the

51

sheepman. And it was then that Sorrell bluntly told Ordway, "Let those sheep stray, and there'll be men up here with rifles."

Kindred slowly turned to face the man once more as Ordway breathed in a quavering, furious voice, "Try that! Just try it and someone gets hurt. It won't be —"

With no warning whatsoever, Sorrell that instant stepped in on the sheepman and with a wickedly fast blow hit him full on the jaw.

Ordway was reeling backward against the wall as Kindred, acting purely on outraged instinct, took two reaching strides in on Sorrell, pushing the man away with a hard jab to shoulder.

Kindred was standing with his back to the onlookers as Sorrell went into a slight crouch, dropping a shoulder. Kindred was certain then that the man was about to hit him. And he was ready and wanting to slug this out.

All at once a driving weight slammed against his back. A pair of arms reached around to pin his elbows to his sides. The next instant Ben Olds lunged in front of him, drew back a fist and hit him a glancing blow on the mouth.

The pain of that fist smashing against his lips was blazing across Kindred's consciousness as the Wineglass foreman said tonelessly, "No one treats Mr. Sorrell that way, Kindred! No one!"

There was a wicked look of gloating in Olds' pale grey eyes. The hard grip pinning Kindred's arms made him wince at the pressure of an elbow against the Colt in his belt, the feel of the weapon driving home a sense of helpless rage in him as Sorrell's man drew back an arm to strike again.

Kindred stiffened against that powerful hold from behind. He lifted his boots and kicked with all his strength as Olds moved in on him. His heels caught the man viciously and square above the belt, drove him lurching backward into Sorrell. Olds groaned in agony, face paling as he retched. And for a split-second Kindred and the man who held him were overbalanced and nearly falling.

Then, as Kindred caught himself, Olds' right hand suddenly slashed his slicker open to make a fast reach to the handle of a holstered gun at his thigh.

That instant Grace Hill's spare figure lunged in between Kindred and Sorrell's man. Taking a step toward Olds, she said in a voice scalding with scorn:

"You gutless coward! Put that gun away!"

# TWO

Over the momentary, taut silence following Grace Hill's words, Frank Sorrell burst out ominously, "Listen, Grace! You keep —"

"I listen when you and this hardcase of yours cool down." The woman cut him off uncompromisingly. "Have a man held while you hit him, will you, Olds? He should've kicked your ugly face in. And you, Frank Sorrell! Laying down the law to this poor devil when his luck's turned. The two of you ought to hide your faces."

"Amen!"

It was Doctor Codrick who had inserted this word of quiet agreement. And now Sorrell regarded the man in outright surprise, afterward giving Olds a sidelong glance, telling him tartly, "Forget it, Ben."

He eyed Grace Hill once more. "Maybe we were a little hasty," he admitted with startling mildness. Nodding in Kindred's direction then, he added, "Turn him loose, Blake."

Kindred felt the hold of the man behind leave his waist. He eased warily back until he was standing beside Ordway at the car's wall, breathing hard, running his tongue over swollen lips and tasting the saltiness of blood.

Then Grace Hill was moving from in front of Ben Olds, asking, testily, "Isn't there something you could all be doing outside?"

Olds' hate-filled glance had all this while clung to Kindred. And suddenly the arrogance of that glance hardened a core of indignation in Kindred at having been so easily manhandled. Knowing what the consequences might be, he was nonetheless going to make certain that something was understood here.

Deliberately, sure that Olds was watching him, he reached up with left hand and unbuttoned his coat in a gesture that had its plain meaning. Then, staring at the man as his coat fell open, very aware of the .45's weight solidly nudging his hipbone, he drawled, "Olds, you were about to try something. Go ahead with it."

There was a hurried movement behind Olds as men stepped out of line. Kindred had time to see the Wineglass man's pale eyes open wide in either startlement or fear before Grace Hill came quickly between them once more.

"No you don't!" she said sharply. "One

man gone to his Maker's enough for one day."

"Step aside, Grace." Kindred's hard stare didn't leave Olds as the woman glanced quickly around at him in alarm. She was confused, frightened, and he edged sideward now, out of line with her, afterward saying tonelessly, "Get on with it, Olds."

Frank Sorrell stated uncertainly, "Here, you two! We can settle this . . ." his words trailing off as he realized that neither man was paying him the slightest attention.

For the length of time it took Jeff Kindred to draw in a slow breath and start exhaling, not a man in the car moved. Then all at once Ben Olds' glance wavered, fell away. He turned abruptly and roughly pushed between two men blocking his way to the waist-high hole in the car's roof. Blake, the one who had held Kindred, followed him. In another moment the two were gone.

Kindred was feeling an angry, restless frustration, at the same time sensing the impact Olds' backing down must be having on Sorrell, the face of the man being temporarily confused, off-guard. Taking advantage of that, he eyed Sorrell to say flatly, "What goes on inside Ladder wire is my lookout, no one else's. Ordway's welcome to graze his sheep here till they can freight him out. He won't need a pen. He won't have to buy feed."

Frank Sorrell's blocky face went momentarily slack with astonishment before it reddened in indignation. It appeared that he was about to speak. But then, looking at the others to take in their wary yet faintly hostile regard, his expression took on an impassiveness as he stared past Kindred to the corner of the car.

"Catherine, what's Noah to say to this notion of sheep fouling his grass?" he asked.

The girl's deliberate answer came at once, her tone edged with a quiet dislike. "This man didn't ask to be stranded here. We'll make the best of it, do as Jeff says."

A hesitant, low mutter of agreement came from several of the onlookers. Frank Sorrell heard it. His look hardened, once again taking on that familiar, cold arrogance. "I have a long memory, a very long one," he stated. He put his disdainful stare on Ordway then. "You've been lucky to land among friends, sheepman. But there's a fence off north of here you'd better stay wide of. My fence."

He stood there a measurable interval, letting the weight of his stony glance bear on Fred Ordway. Then he wheeled and strode across to the jagged opening in the car and stepped outside.

Kindred let his breath go in a slow, relieved sigh, turning to take in William Codrick's spare, delighted smile and Grace Hill's disbelieving bewilderment. But it was the gentle, wondering look Catherine Horn gave him that registered most strongly upon his awareness.

Ledge's main street lay bathed in bright sunlight the next morning as the courthouse clock struck the hour of ten. Four doors down the street, the sound of the bell made Frank Sorrell, in his office over the bank, look around at the tall floor clock, the hands of which indicated the time to be four minutes after ten.

He gave an irritated grunt and took out his pocket watch, seeing that its time precisely matched the clock's. "Why don't they fix it?" he muttered, afterward directing his attention to a ledger lying open before him on the desk.

This scanning of the bank's accounts was a regular chore of Sorrell's. Though he had repeatedly refused to serve on the bank's board of directors, he was by far its heaviest depositor. As such, the board had long ago prevailed upon him to give the balance sheet his expert attention.

He closed the book now, rose and reached

down his hat from the antelope-antlered rack on the wall. As an afterthought he took a stogie from an applewood box on his desk, meticulously trimmed and lit it, then put the ledger under his arm and went down the outside covered stairway.

It was typical of him to waste hardly a second in his brief stop at the bank. He walked the length of the short corridor before the two cages, opened the door lettered *President*, laid the ledger on the polished desk inside and told the man who quickly rose from the chair behind the desk, "Morning, John. No sense bothering to make inquiries about that collateral Bledsoe's putting up for his loan. It's only fair and so's he. So don't go through with it."

He turned, ignoring the other's, "But, Frank, how's Bledsoe going to last if —" his closing of the door cutting off the man's words.

After leaving the bank, Sorrell was striding along the awninged plank walk in front of Harmer's store when a pair of horsemen approaching from downstreet took his eye. Recognizing Ben Olds as one of these, he came to a stand at the walk's edge, once looking casually around and tipping his hat to a sunbonneted woman who gave him a nervous smile and said, "A fine day for a change, Mr. Sorrell."

"Fine it is, Mrs. Ballew." Sorrell's tone was courteous but aloof, and he gave the woman but a brief attention.

Ben Olds saw him waiting there and brought his horse obliquely over the puddled street, with a brief word sending the other man straight on. Olds shortly drew rein beyond the sagging rail close by, giving Sorrell a respectful nod, Sorrell at once asking, "How does it look up there this morning?"

"Quiet, Mr. Sorrell. As good as a sheep camp can, I reckon. Last night Kindred and old Grace helped this herder throw up a rope corral." Eyeing Sorrell uneasily, Olds growled, "Damn that old she cat for stoppin' me from —"

"A good thing she did," Sorrell interrupted coolly. Then all at once he was asking, "Why're you afraid of Kindred, Ben?"

The other's face flushed. "You think that was any place to throw lead?"

"You started to. While Blake was holding him for you." Sorrell let the words sink in a long moment. Then: "He had you scared, made you eat crow. Why would you let him?"

Olds' glance wavered, and he drawled sullenly, "There never was the day when I was scared of that Kindred or any other man."

Sorrell smiled coldly, pointedly, before he said, "Your affair, Ben. But go on about the sheep. What's doing up there today?"

"They're feeding off south across the meadow," Olds replied, obviously relieved at the subject having been changed. "I left Blake up there to keep an eye out."

"Good." Sorrell stood a moment in thought before continuing, "Better have two men watching. If the sheep work our way, you're to let them come. If they get through the fence, you're still to let them come till they're far enough beyond the wire to count. Then you'll shoot them down. Night's the likely time for it to happen, so you'd better stay up there with whoever's watching."

Olds' look narrowed. "Suppose this bird kicks up a ruckus if we cut down his critters?"

The rancher stared aloofly at his man. "Don't bother me with having to think out every move you're to make. If he doesn't toe the line, make him toe it."

"Then I got a free hand in this?"

Frank Sorrell gave his man a bland look, saying crisply, "That's all, Ben."

Olds' glance held Sorrell's only briefly. He seemed on the point of protesting, but finally pulled his horse out from the rail, drawling, "You'll hear from me," and went on up the street.

Over the next hour and a half, Frank Sorrell followed a morning ritual that varied only slightly from day to day. Precisely at ten-thirty he appeared at the barber shop, where the chair was being held for him though two other customers were waiting. After his neck-shave and beard trim he walked on up to the cross street and took it to the station, spending twenty minutes with Kemp, the station agent.

From the station, Sorrell walked on up to his feed mill, where he spent nearly an hour with the manager. It was getting on toward noon, too late to go back to his office, by the time he left the mill, so he turned away from the stores and walked leisurely up the drying, black dirt path leading past the houses along the upper street.

Made restless by these unlooked-for spare minutes, his thoughts turned to that uncomfortable interval yesterday afternoon when first Grace Hill, then Kindred, had outfaced him in the boxcar up the mountain. He felt the blood pounding in his head at the recollection of how thoroughly Kindred had humbled him. Not many times in his life had he had to give ground to anyone.

And the fact of his having done so yesterday irked him deeply.

The word of his set-to with the man must have spread widely by now, though as he considered the stand he had taken he failed to see how he had been anything but right. The presence of sheep up there near the pass just might give a few homesteaders and nesters a wrong notion. This was cattle country, and cattle country it would stay if he had anything to say about it, which he did.

He might also have something to say about Kindred, about the man's future. He had no sooner started considering this, though, than he came within sight of his mansard-roofed brick house. And, as always when he glimpsed it on a fair day such as this, he was gripped by a nostalgia and a measure of quiet grief that made him forget all but one thing.

The house, though large and handsome, stood as a monument to the only failure in Frank Sorrell's life. It had been built some fourteen years ago for a woman he had intended marrying, built for her and planned for her. For several years, until he had himself chiseled it out, one of the front cornerstones had even borne her name, Lorna, along with the date 1873. But she had never lived in the house. Shortly after its completion she had disappeared, having given him no warning of her going, not even a written word of explanation.

He still professed complete ignorance of what had happened to her, and of why she had gone, though one of several men he had secretly hired to trace her had brought him word of a young woman answering his fiancée's description having been seen aboard a stage, in the company of a man, headed east through New Utopia the day after her disappearance. He had always labeled as a coincidence the boom-town's loss of a young and handsome gambler a day or so before the girl's sudden disappearance.

The realization that he had failed miserably in loving and holding the woman of his choice had come eventually, marking the beginning of a hardness in him that had grown stronger as time went on. The house had stood empty the next three years, its windows and doors boarded up, its grounds rank with weeds. It had taken some patient and hard-headed logic on the part of his maiden sister, Harriet, to make him realize that in leaving the house empty he was only flaunting a grief he insisted he didn't feel.

He and Harriet had moved into the place just one week from the day of her casual mention of having overheard someone refer to the house as ". . . Frank Sorrell's empty hope chest." He and Harriet had lived in the house ever since. And over these intervening years Sorrell had halfway come to believe that it had been some other girl aboard the stage, that somehow Lorna had died, alone and mysteriously, while still adoring him.

Today his thoughts of his vanished bride-to-be were remote, however, as he came to the brick wall fronting the house and admired Hattie's neatly cultivated beds of marigolds, petunias and wild asters lining the other side of the ornate wrought-iron fence. On his way through the gate he picked a corn flower and was putting it in the buttonhole of his coat lapel as he climbed the porch steps.

His somber mood of a few minutes ago was gone now. He tossed his hat onto a chair in the hallway and called out cheerfully, "Dinner ready, Hattie?"

Waiting for her answer, he hesitated in mid-stride. That answer didn't come, though he could hear her moving about in the kitchen. He started back there, calling more loudly, "What's for dinner, girl?"

Still he got no answer. A scowl slowly gathered on his face then as he went on past the dining room arch to the open kitchen door. He stopped there, looking across at his sister as she stood before the stove using a spoon to turn a panful of fried potatoes.

He balefully eyed her straight back a moment before querying, "Now what's wrong?"

"I'm in no mood to talk about it, Frank. Get washed."

He watched her cross to the sink, his scowl deepening. Oddly this moment, with the sunlight streaming through the window against her deep black hair and etching her fine, regular profile so sharply, he was thinking, *She's still a damn' good looking woman,* though none of that flattering thought tinged his words as he told her, "Get it off your chest, whatever it is."

She turned abruptly and folded her arms, leaning back against the pump at the sink. "Martha Kemp called this morning, Frank."

"So? And what did the old gossip have to tell you?"

"Her man was up there at the train wreck last night."

A question was in Sorrell's glance. "Go on."

"Frank, is there anything but snow melt pumping through that heart of yours? Or have you any heart at all?"

Sorrell felt his face turn hot, for Harriet was the one person in this town, anywhere for that matter, who could without fail humble him when she chose. He loved this woman and he was quite aware of her being in no small way responsible for his material success. Five years his senior, she was shrewd, kind and generous, much respected.

Realization of this took some of his testiness away as he asked, "Now what have I done?"

She eyed him belittlingly a moment before replying. "At times you're like a youngster who's stolen a pie. You know what you've done, or tried to do. I'm ashamed of you, Frank. Ashamed, hear?"

Sorrell was about to argue, to deny any knowledge of what she was inferring. But then his better judgment made him say, "What would you have done? Invited the man to drive his sheep down onto our place where it'll be easier on him if a good freeze comes along?"

"No. I'd simply have given him to understand that sheep aren't wanted in this country. That he's to move out the first chance he has. You belittled yourself, Frank Sorrell, by fighting with him, by striking him. You're a bigger man than that. Or so I'd thought."

Sorrell was angry, but he was also

ashamed. And as a real chagrin cut into him, he said bitterly, "It makes no difference to you that Kindred threw in with this man?"

"Threw in with him? He did not. He simply wouldn't take advantage of the poor soul. And I hear he also showed Ben Olds up for the bully he is." Pausing a moment, Harriet added quietly, "You were looking for trouble, Frank. As you do sometimes. The good Lord knows I'm glad Mrs. Hill and Kindred had the gumption to stop you. You made a thorough devil of yourself, the same as you're doing in kicking those people around about this toll road. And you can listen to this!"

He stood angrily waiting until she said in a quavering, furious way, "If I hear that you're thinking up ways of making it hard for Kindred, and for Cathy and Noah because of this, I'll move my things from this house and never set foot in it again. Now get out of here."

Sorrell turned sharply away with a bewildered shake of the head, "As though I didn't have enough to think about without this."

No reply came from the kitchen as he went along the hallway and turned up the stairs. He was muttering, swearing as he washed at the stand in his big upstairs bedroom. He had expected that this interval would let him get a grip on his anger. But it was still alive in him when he came downstairs and went to the dining room.

He noticed that Hattie's place at the table's other end wasn't laid. Presently she came in from the kitchen, setting a plate of food, a cup and saucer and a pot of coffee in front of him.

"Sit there and stew in your own juice," she told him. "I'm going next door to talk with Mrs. Cauble till you're out of the house."

Hugh Codrick, in addition to Frank Sorrell, had spent a nerve-wracking morning, though in a lesser degree. Last night it had taken the lawyer nearly six hours to drive from the cabin above Gap across the pass and down to Ledge. Then, on his way from the livery, he had happened to notice the hotel lobby still brightly lighted and a group of men gathered there. Curiosity had taken him in to learn of the sheep train wreck, so that it was nearly one o'clock when he finally reached home.

This morning, tired, behind in his work, he had been forced to endure patiently the complaints and arguments of two homesteaders from up near Frenchy Duval's who were incensed over losing their layouts if Sorrell's toll road suit was successful. This interview left him so crowded for time that he almost decided against going home during the noon hour, though the fact of his not having seen his father the past two days, and his real anxiety over the doctor's health, finally did take him wearily down the street.

On entering the house he found the office doorway closed. Supposing that his father must be busy with a patient, he was starting back along the hallway when William Codrick called from beyond the closed door, "That you, Hugh? Come in."

Hugh went on into the room to find the old man alone, standing before glass-fronted cabinet at the far wall. And as he appeared his parent said, "Mind closing the door?"

Hugh did so, frowning as the medico took a bottle from the back of one of the cabinet's shelves. "Why the secrecy, dad?"

"Just don't like the idea of someone coming in and finding me dosing myself with this stuff."

Recognizing the bottle then, the lawyer asked worriedly, "The pain's worse today?"

"No worse, no better."

"Then why start on the chloral hydrate before suppertime?"

The medico made no reply until he had

carefully poured some liquid from the bottle into a small graduate. "This isn't for the pain, Hugh. Nothing can touch that. But I need a couple hours' rest." Looking around at his son, he added, "Couldn't get to sleep last night because you hadn't come home. You were late."

A strong annoyance was in Codrick as he said, "I was lucky to get here at all. Had to borrow a buggy in Gap. Then I saw this bunch in the hotel and had to go in and find out all about the wreck. But you shouldn't have worried. I'm dry behind the ears."

"So you are." William Codrick turned away to fill the graduate from a flask of water. Then he downed the mixture, afterward shaking his head ruefully to say, "To think I'd wind up my days depending on a drug."

"If it helps, take it."

"That's one way of looking at it." The doctor picked up the bottle, frowning at it, saying musingly, "Must be taking more of this than I'd realized." With a shrug, he returned bottle and graduate to the cabinet's shelf. "So you've heard about the slide?"

The lawyer nodded. "They say you were there."

"I was. Wouldn't have missed it even if

it wasn't too good for me." His look turning grave, the medico stated, "That was a fine thing Kindred did."

"What? Telling Sorrell off?" There was a faint sarcasm in Hugh's tone.

"No, wasn't thinking of that. Though it was good to be in on, too. I was thinking of his digging for the engine when the others were so sure it was hopeless. He saved a man's life."

The lawyer nodded, grudgingly admitting, "He knows his mind certainly. Once in a while that pays off."

William Codrick eyed him speculatively. "It always pays off, Hugh. Always."

Uncomfortable before his parent's stare, Hugh shrugged, saying, "I hear Cathy was there."

"So she was. She was here last evening when Pete Ballew came to get me. She'd come to see you. I may be wrong, but she gave me the impression she was worried about something."

"Worried," the lawyer echoed blandly, though carefully. "What could be worrying her?"

"Can't think of a thing. She was lovely. As lovely as your mother used to be, so I told her. You're a fortunate man."

Once again an annoyance rose in Hugh

Codrick. He said a trifle aloofly, "Don't count my chickens for me, dad."

"But the time's not far off when you can count them, I hope." The doctor was regarding his son solemnly. "I should like to see it happen in my lifetime, Hugh. It would please me if you didn't delay too long. There may not be much time."

"That's no way to talk."

"Perhaps. But now and then certain things have to be said."

The lawyer was still feeling that irritation as he went to the door. "I'd hoped you'd feel like coming along for a bite to eat."

"Not today. I'll rest till about two if I can. Maud's coming and she can get me something after I'm up."

On his way back up the street, Hugh Codrick was sullenly and angrily thinking back upon his parent's blunt comments regarding Cathy. Though he had a strong hope of one day marrying Cathy, he had decided that the time wasn't yet propitious for mentioning that hope to her, and it irritated him to have his father assume what he had.

One other remark of the doctor's had irked him. The elder Codrick's slighting mention of Frank Sorrell, coupled with his praise of Jeff Kindred, had been exceedingly annoying. Hugh wondered just now what his father would say when the full details of his part in Sorrell's scheming on the new toll road became known. And an intolerance was in him at the prospect of having to explain his reasoning in having taken the case, which had been that, in order to keep Sorrell as his most valued client, he had to run the risk of offending a few people of lesser importance.

He was approaching the wide walk awning in front of Harmer's store, somberly thinking of all this, when a voice called from above, "Codrick!"

He glanced quickly up to the head of his office stairway to see a tall, thin man standing in the doorway. A hard wariness at once gripped him. He slowed his stride. Trying to be casual about it, he glanced up the street, then down it. And as he turned up the stairway he was relieved at being fairly certain that no passers-by had been close enough to hear him being hailed.

The man above had stepped back into the lawyer's office. Codrick, as he entered, snapped, "Haven't I warned you to be careful about this?"

The other, middle-aged and greying, gave him a stare of cold dislike before answering quietly, "I didn't shout. No one was in sight. And no one saw me come up here."

Codrick leaned back against the door, turning the key in the lock. "All right, Semple, we'll keep our voices down. Why're you here?"

"Why do you think? She's brought me ore for another assay. Just this morning."

The lawyer's hostility at once faded before a look of eagerness. "How did it turn out?"

Instead of immediately replying, Semple paced slowly to the street window and stood a moment fingering an elk-tooth charm hanging from a heavy gold chain stretched across his vest. Then shortly he was saying in an outraged way, "It's a shameful thing I'm doing. I don't like any part of it."

"You don't?" Codrick smiled faintly, arrogantly.

"I don't. I want to know how long you'll hold this over me."

"Not much longer."

"But how much longer?"

"That's for me to decide," Codrick stated silkily.

"That answer won't do, Codrick. I want an understanding between us. I want it here and now!"

"You do?" The lawyer laughed. "And if you don't get it?"

"Then I'm . . ."

Codrick waited for the man to finish.

When Semple didn't go on, he drawled, "Careful. You wouldn't like it if I turned over this new evidence on Tadd to the judge."

Semple's strong face took on an undisguised loathing and contempt. "Yes, I believe you'd do it. Even though you know Tadd was just a strongheaded young fool taken in by two older men."

"All I know is that your boy was an accessory to murder and armed robbery. Even if all he did was hold the horses. Had I known it at the time, I wouldn't have defended him. I also know that Wells Fargo, if they had the information I've run onto since, would hunt Tadd down if he was as far away as Mexico." Codrick had spoken deliberately. Now, his voice not losing its edge, he asked, "So we understand each other?"

The other sighed wearily. "I'm afraid we do."

"Then let's have it. How did the assay run?"

"It was hard to believe. I should judge a ton of such ore would produce at least nine hundred dollars in gold."

The catch in Hugh Codrick's breathing was plainly audible. "No!"

Semple stood there eyeing him stonily,

waiting. In another moment Codrick was asking, "You're sure about this?"

"I'm not often mistaken," Semple answered tonelessly.

Codrick paced slowly across to his desk now and took the chair behind it. Abruptly a look of cunning was in his eyes. "You know every shaft and gallery in the Difficult, Semple. Exactly what part of the mine would you say this ore came from?"

The assayer's look was puzzled. "Why should that matter?"

"Because some of those galleries in the Difficult cross the fence line and run under Wineglass land. When they were working the mine, Grace and her husband paid lease money to both Sorrell and John Horn. I want to know exactly where Grace got this ore."

Semple shook his head. "I've seen rock out of a stope on D level something like this. Which would put it well inside the Ladder lease. But I can't swear that this is the same."

Codrick appeared faintly disappointed, though his tone was quiet, even, as he said, "It would go hard with Tadd if you ever hinted to Grace Hill that she's onto something good, Semple."

"You needn't repeat your threats. I'll simply tell her that there's a trace of gold, but not enough. And may God forgive me."

"And you also know it would go hard with Tadd if you should start snooping around up there, don't you?"

Utter contempt was in the other's glance now. He simply nodded, nothing more.

"Then you can go now." Codrick tilted his head toward the door.

That morning, shortly before five o'clock, Jeff Kindred had ridden his buckskin mule in out of the cold, thinning darkness beyond the blazing chuck-wagon fire to surprise the men who stood huddled close to the leaping flames, bundled in their warmest outfits as they finished a heavy breakfast.

Men from all the outfits along the slopes were here, had been for a week now, working the hills and the flats on the late fall roundup, and the first one to see Kindred called, "Here's the bird we been lookin' for. Posey, make him the goat on the wood haul today," his tone bantering rather than sarcastic. And another said, "Jeff, you called the right turn, waitin' till the weather cleared." Others came out with salty but nonetheless good-natured remarks as Kindred dismounted alongside the camp boss.

"Put me to work, Posey," he said.

The man gave him a sober, questioning look. "Didn't find Noah there when you got back?" At Kindred's shake of the head, Posey swore soundly, adding, "We hear you come in handy up at the wreck." Then, sensing he had made Kindred uncomfortable, he quickly went on, "Well, we can sure use you today. There's a jag of wild stuff hid in that brush through the breaks up north. You can have three men to work it. But get something hot in you before you pull out."

By midday, Kindred and the other three could count twenty-nine animals gathered from the rough tangle of brush-choked country they were working. By four o'clock, when a rider loped toward them across the flats, they were scouring the last of the thickets to the south.

It was one of the others, not Kindred, who first saw the approaching horseman and called, "Here's the missin' member, Jeff."

Kindred brought his mule on through a high, heavy clump of oak brush nearby, reining in to glance the way the other was looking. He at once recognized Noah's paint horse, now something like half a mile away, and relief was blended with the anger that hit him. His companion, evidently catching his expression, said, "You go on and see

79

him. The three of us can handle the rest of this."

Kindred nodded his thanks, sending the mule on in a line that would intercept Noah. He rode slowly, his anger gradually quieting before a deep thankfulness, for last night after his talk with Cathy at the wreck he had begun thinking that something really ominous must lie behind his partner's long absence.

He rode on for several hundred yards, finally halting at the edge of a deep wash to wait as Noah brought his animal across the still-muddy depression. And by the time the other put the paint into a slogging climb toward him he was smiling a genuine welcome.

He drawled, "Behold, the wandering son," as Noah came alongside, but then he was instantly regretting the levity of his words as he took in his partner's bridling glance.

"All right, read me the lesson, parson."

That acid comment, along with the bitter stare so unlike any expression he had ever before seen on Noah's face, surprised Kindred into saying, "You been drinkin' from the wrong label, man. What's got into you?"

"Go on, let's have it." Noah's tone grated with a dry sarcasm. "Tell me what a big help I've been this last week."

"No one said anything about that. You're back, which is the main thing."

"Back, yes. But not for long." Noah's angry stare thinned a trifle as he asked, "Bring anything back in your pockets?"

Kindred shook his head. "Not even as much as I left with."

"Then you can have it all in one bundle, Jeff." Noah's voice was brittle, hurried. "I've played out my string here. I'm through, finished. Don't ask why, but I'm unloading my share of the outfit to the first taker. To you or Cathy if I can. If not to you then to some man Codrick says he's got lined up, someone you may not know about yet."

"I know about him," Kindred quietly inserted.

"But I'm pulling out," Noah insisted. "Understand?"

There was an unmistakable edge of panic in his tone, his look. Kindred, grasping that without even beginning to understand it, protested, "Start from the beginning, kid. Tell me —"

"That's all I tell you," Noah interrupted, glancing nervously beyond Kindred toward the men working the small bunch of cattle in the distance. "Something's happened since you've been gone. Something that means I leave here and head plenty far away. I shouldn't even be seen here like this. But I'll take my chance on gatherin' up a few things at the layout and then go in to see Cathy. I'll try and leave her some word on where I can be reached."

Kindred sat staring incredulously at the man, their glances locked for a long moment. Finally, his expression softening, Noah spoke again. "I know what I'm doing to you, Jeff. And to Cathy. But it has to be this way. I'm no damned good, haven't been for so long I hate to think back on it. You'll be better off without me."

"That's like claimin' I'm better off without my right arm."

The bitterness of the smile that came to Noah's face then shocked Kindred. "A right arm's of some use to a man. I haven't been any use to you. Or to myself."

Noah lifted rein now and turned the paint away. Though Kindred sensed the futility of more words, he doggedly stated, "Kid, you've got friends. Me, to begin with. Let us help straighten this out, whatever's wrong. I'll go all the way with you."

"I know you would," Noah replied gently. "But it's no go, Jeff. I asked for this and I'll take what I have comin'."

Touching his animal with the spur then,

he said, "Luck to you," as he ran his horse away.

Some two hours after Kindred had watched Noah ride out of sight, Hugh Codrick ate a leisurely meal in the small hotel dining room, lingering afterward at the table to relish a cigar. He now and then glanced at the clock over the lobby door, watching its hands creep past the hour of six-thirty in the knowledge that Reno was probably already waiting in the alley below his office.

But he was in no hurry. For Frank Sorrell was eating a solitary meal at one of the corner tables, and he intended catching the man's eye and going across to have a word with him before leaving. He wondered idly why Sorrell should be eating here tonight, knowing that the man's sister rarely went out of an evening. Yet his curiosity over that was soon forgotten as the minutes passed without the other looking in his direction.

Finally, at forty-five minutes past the hour, a sudden impatience made him rise and saunter over to Sorrell's table. " 'Evening, Mr. Sorrell. How goes it?"

Sorrell gave him a frowning stare, plainly irritated at the interruption. "Fair enough."

"Just wanted you to know that the case is shaping up nicely," Codrick said, wishing now that he hadn't come across here.

Sorrell's frown deepened. "What case?"

"Getting that tax condemned land for the road."

"Oh, that." Sorrell sat several moments staring at the wall beyond the table, at length looking up once more. "I may've had a change of mind on that," he unexpectedly announced. "Don't know that I want to go through with it."

Codrick could scarcely believe his hearing. "But the judgment is practically certain to be in your favor, sir."

"I know, I know." The older man lifted a hand from the table's edge in a spare gesture of annoyance, crisply adding, "Now's no time to discuss it. Come see me in the morning. I may want to drop the thing altogether. No sense crowding those folks off their land just because the poor devils can't lay hands on any money."

On the point of protesting further, the lawyer thought better of it. "Just as you say, sir. Would ten o'clock suit?"

Sorrell merely nodded and gave his attention to his eating once more, leaving Codrick no choice beyond saying, "I'll be there," and leaving.

Codrick was out of sorts, tired and more than a little annoyed as he went out onto the darkened street and started along it. Though he was familiar enough with Frank Sorrell's brusque manner, it galled him to be treated as an underling, almost as a servant. He couldn't fathom the reasons for the man having taken this unexpected attitude on the toll road, though as he thought back he could well remember how, on agreeing to take the case, he had been awed by Sorrell's indifference to the fate of the people whose land he proposed acquiring for next to nothing.

It had been his recognizing of this callous attitude in Sorrell, plus an awareness of the man's shrewdness and uncanny foresight generally in business dealings, that had several weeks ago inspired Codrick to arrive at a bold decision. Using Sorrell as an example, trying to pattern his thinking after him, the lawyer had furtively begun taking steps toward accomplishing something that had until then been no more than a wild, wishful imagining.

It was unsettling now to think that a man as strong-minded as Frank Sorrell would suddenly turn about and act in a way counter to his original intentions. A man should never let his emotions sway him once he had set out upon such a project as the toll road. And Codrick, abruptly seeing this basic truth, at once forgot his irritation in the face of the realization that he was in this respect a stronger man even than Sorrell.

So a warped pride and a heady conceit were in him some moments later as he walked the length of Harmer's store-front and turned into the head of the broad passageway out of which his office stairway climbed. He was edging cautiously into the pitch blackness, reaching for the railing, when a voice spoke quietly out of the blackness close ahead:

"You said six-thirty."

The lawyer froze in startlement, involuntarily taking a backward step before he caught himself. It was a moment before he could put down his wary surprise and say, "Couldn't be helped, Reno."

"I been here since long before then."

"I said it couldn't be helped." The knowledge of this man having made him appear somewhat ridiculous a moment ago made Codrick add sharply, "Thought I told you to wait out back."

"What difference, here or there? No one knows I'm around."

The lawyer checked an angry rejoinder, realizing the absurdity of the attitude he was taking. He could vaguely make out Reno's broad shape leaning indolently against the stairway joist, thumbs hooked in the shell-belt that sagged onto his right thigh. Though he sensed a quality of insolence in that relaxed stand, he nevertheless put a casualness in his tone as he queried, "Anything new for me?"

"Not too much. Got to the mine along about eleven last night and went in the usual way, along that air shaft. Bedded down for a good sleep in one of those holes —"

"Sleep?" the lawyer exploded, afterward glancing apprehensively toward the walk as he heard someone coming along the street. When he went on it was in a tone barely above a whisper, "You weren't there to sleep, man!"

"Should I of set waitin' for seven or eight hours?" Reno saw Codrick lift a hand to silence him and, listening a moment to the step approaching along the street, added, "He's on the far side, whoever he is." He went on in a normal low tone then. "I sleep like a cat and I was hid good. Sure enough, she roused me when she come past with her lantern early this mornin'."

"You followed her?"

"Best I could. Understand, you can't walk right on that old coot's heels. Not with them tunnels throwin' echoes the way they do. I shed my boots and took out after her. Only she turned into a side gallery and give me a bad few minutes."

"Go on, go on," the lawyer breathed impatiently.

"Well, by the time I'd felt my way into the drift, she'd clumb out of it up a side shaft. I was lucky. Spotted her light just after she stepped off the ladder above."

"What level was that?"

"B level," Reno answered quietly. "I give her maybe a minute's start and went on up. Then's when she had me."

"You mean you lost her?"

"Not exactly. But I didn't never really find her again neither. There's this damn water pourin' into the drift she went along. I think it's the north one. Anyways, it sets up such a racket you can't hear nothin' else. I hot-footed it after her fast as I could and saw her light way ahead of me once, toward where the water spills in. Then I walked smack into the falls. God A'mighty, did I get soaked!"

Codrick let his breath go audibly in a baffled, angry way. "So she gave you the slip?"

"You couldn't rightly call it that," Reno answered in aggravating casualness. "I backed clear of the spray, knowin' she couldn't have gone no further because it blocks the whole gallery. My matches was still dry, so I lit some and worked my way back, lookin' for side drifts. There are two that cut left from the main —"

"Left when you're facing which way?" Codrick cut in. "This is important, Reno."

"Facin' back the way you come, your back to the falls."

"I can check that on the plan," the lawyer said. "Go on. What happened next?"

"You got a plan of the Difficult?" Reno asked. "Get it. I could save us a lot of time if I saw the whole layout."

"Never mind," Codrick said quickly, deciding against the risk of taking this man up to his office. "I can remember how it looks. I'll be able to locate it. Go ahead."

"There ain't much more to tell. These two drifts was short ones. I walked 'em both out. She wasn't in either one."

"She had to be."

"So I thought. But she wasn't."

Codrick stood silent a long moment, annoyed, feeling let down. At length he asked, "You waited for her to come out?"

"Yeah. She wasn't in there long. She come back say in about another hour totin' a heavy sack. Went straight back down the ladder and on out. This afternoon she rode down the cut toward the town road with

89

the sack tied on behind her hull."

"Probably brought another sample in to be assayed. Damn!"

"Did the best I could, Codrick."

"I know." The lawyer was silent a moment, then said, "Well, you'll have to go back and try again. Only this time wait for her on B level and keep her in sight. If this water makes all the noise you say, you can stay closer to her. Now here's something else, something you can do on your way back up there tonight." And Codrick went on talking, his voice low, intent.

Reno interrupted him only once, to ask, "For how much?"

"Say five dollars extra. The whole thing won't take you over two hours at the most."

"Say ten."

Codrick caught himself on the point of arguing, thinking of Frank Sorrell this moment, knowing the man wouldn't quibble under a like circumstance. So he said, "Ten it is," and went on talking.

Finally, some two minutes later, he finished by asking, "Got it all straight?"

"Straight as a string."

Codrick turned toward the stairway, nodding. "Then that's all. Except that you'd better be here tomorrow night at the same time."

"Just one more thing," Reno drawled. He waited until the lawyer had swung to face him once more before continuing, "This thing seems to be shapin' up to something big. I been thinkin' maybe you ought to cut me in for part of it."

A cold rage instantly hit Codrick. Yet the next moment he knew that he must somehow play this man along. He needed Reno badly, needed him now more than he had at any time during the past days. So, very carefully, he said, "Cut you in how? A share?"

Reno shook his head. "No. I'm the kind that's likely to pull stakes and want to head somewheres else. I'd feel less tied down if you settled with me for just one chunk of money."

"But we don't know yet how this is to turn out," Codrick hedged. "We've barely got the thing started."

"So we have," Reno agreed. "But I wouldn't be hard to please."

"Then name a figure," the lawyer said warily. "I can either meet it or turn it down."

Reno stood silent for several seconds, at length drawling, "Couple years ago I run across a nice little filly down El Paso way. Mexican girl. There's a layout off there in the hills I could pick up for say eight or nine hundred dollars. A man's got to get settled down sooner or later. I could do me the whole she-bang on a thousand. I'd call it quits on this deal for that much."

Codrick laughed dryly. "Who wouldn't? This isn't that big, man."

"If it isn't, then you're over-payin' me."

The lawyer was suddenly impatient at this sparring between them. But he was also being very careful. He said, "Tell you what. We aren't sure of anything just yet. Give me another week and we may be. Meantime, I want to be able to count on you."

"You can count on me all right. Only I'm gettin' the itchy foot, thinkin' it won't be too long till I'll be on my way. These are killin' winters up here and I'd just as soon miss this one."

The lawyer nodded, stepping onto the stairway now. "It won't take much longer."

He went on up the steps then, in a few seconds glancing down, about to speak again. But Reno was no longer there. The man had either stepped back out of sight into the deeper shadows or was gone and Codrick felt a moment's uneasiness as he climbed the stairway, a strange apprehension in him until he had unlocked his door and was inside the office.

He pulled down the blinds on the two street windows and locked the door before lighting the lamp, afterward going to a deal cabinet behind the desk and pulling the bottom drawer out onto the floor. Reaching up inside the opening, he pulled four tacks from the top of the cabinet lining, drawing out a large, folded sheet of paper as it fell free.

Unfolding the sheet, he took it to the desk and spread it out flat, his glance cursorily taking in the legend along its top. DIFFICULT MINE, LEDGE OPERATION, JOSHUA BROS., before he began running a finger along the elevation profile.

In a few more seconds his finger was tracing out the line of the B level north gallery that ended with the marking, *Falls. Drain Fissure.* His hand was trembling then as it followed the two wavy lines of the drain fissure at a downward angle to join a heavier line he was certain must designate the outer face of the slope, for beyond it was printed, *Elk Creek.*

He breathed a hard sigh a moment later as, well beyond the far margin of the stream marking, he saw a line of crisscrossed pen strokes captioned, *Fence,* and knew it to be Wineglass's boundary.

His relief was so vast that it left him weak. He knew now with no shadow of a doubt that Grace Hill had brought Martin Semple ore from the Ladder lease, not from that portion of the Difficult that lay under Frank Sorrell's land.

A heady elation was rising in him when all at once his frame went rigid at the sound of someone mounting the outside stairway. He wheeled quickly and thrust the plans of the Difficult into the bottom of the cabinet, then shoved the drawer back into place. He hurried noiselessly across the room, hearing those steps approaching the stair head as he quietly eased the key around in the lock.

He was backing away from the door when a knock sounded against it.

# THREE

Some twenty minutes before Hugh Codrick climbed the stairs to his office after his talk with Reno, Jeff Kindred had carried a large box from a store down the street, loaded it into the bed of a buckboard and then driven the rig on up to the bakery, where he tied his team.

A lamp was burning on the bakery's counter, though when he tried the door he found it locked. He rattled the door loudly, afterward knocking the bottle from the pipe he had been smoking. And as he pocketed the pipe and then stood waiting his mood was one of sustained, impotent anger, along with extreme patience.

Some seconds later Cathy came from the rear room, and with a gusty sigh of resignation Kindred reached up and removed his hat, watching the girl as she came from behind the counter.

"You, Jeff," Cathy said on opening the door. Her tone was subdued, and in this poor light her sensitive face wore an expression of utter gravity that made it quite beautiful. "I was hoping to see you."

He stepped on into the room, asking, "Noah's been here?"

She nodded, closing the door. "About half an hour ago." Staring up at him a moment, she murmured lifelessly, "I just can't believe it. He's gone. Without saying why. Without . . ."

When her voice trailed off helplessly, Kindred told her, "That's the way he was with me. Wish I could help you, but I can't."

They stared mutely at one another for several seconds, Cathy finally tilting her head toward the back of the room, saying quietly, "Won't you come on back where we can be more comfortable?"

"I'd better not stay. Got a box of things I'm taking up to Ordway tonight. He's about out of grub."

He was shocked at seeing the lost, numbed look that came to her eyes then. And in another moment she was asking, "What are we going to do, Jeff?"

"Same as we've been doing."

"But you can't run the place on your own."

"I can till spring."

"If they let you," she said resignedly. Her look brightened with anger then, and she said, "Jeff, let's sell the place to Hugh's man. Sell it while we can get a good price. While there's still a chance of your getting something out of it. This has been nothing but a thankless chore for you from the very beginning."

His expression bridled. He shook his head, "I'd rather take the full licking than just half a one, Catherine. If there's to be a licking. The layout means more to me than just getting out from under. It should to you."

"What makes you think it doesn't?" she countered, showing the first real animation he had seen in her tonight. But then there was still that hopeless quality in her tone as she went on, "I'm simply looking at things sanely. We're in debt. The bank will know as well as we that you can't possibly work the place by yourself. Let's don't wait for them to put an end to something we know can't work anyway."

He held a stubborn silence, having spoken his mind, and in several more seconds she was saying gently, "I like you for not wanting to give up. You've been fine all the way through, Jeff. Not only with Noah but with me. But there's a limit to how much you can ask of yourself, how much I can ask."

It unsettled him now to have his strong

awareness of this girl intrude upon his thinking. Whether or not she realized it, there had been a quality of deep affection for him, almost of intimacy, in her look and her words just now. And for a moment he dropped the strictly impersonal manner he had always used with her to say, "Catherine, Ladder's yours. Your home. I'd like to see it stay yours."

Her eyes came wider open. It was as though she was seeing something in him she had never known was there. "You really mean that. You're doing this more for me than you are for yourself."

He felt awkward now at having shown her something he had always been on guard against showing, and he said uneasily, "When you've had the chance to think it over, you'll see it the way I do."

She stood eyeing him in that awed, wondering way a moment longer, as though wanting to be very certain of the thing she had glimpsed in him. Then, shaking her head, she told him, "No, we can't let our feelings decide this. It could never turn out any way but the wrong way for you. I'm so tired of all this, Jeff. I want to forget it, forget what Noah's done."

That same stubborn anger of this afternoon was in Kindred once more. "There's

98

another thing we could try," he told her.

"What is it?"

"Go to Hugh Codrick. Let him —"

"Can't we decide this on our own?"

She spoke with a real annoyance, and this unexpected reaction in her was puzzling Kindred as he explained, "I'm not saying he's to help decide anything. But he's got this man with the offer. Let him go to him and see if he'll buy out Noah's share. That way we'd have something to give the bank, providing Noah agrees."

She regarded him thoughtfully, a look of hope coming slowly alive in her hazel eyes. "That would be all we'd need, wouldn't it? Paying off the rest would be easy."

He was thankful at seeing this reviving of her spirit, and he drawled, "Dead easy."

"Then I'll go see Hugh. Tonight. Right now." She saw him about to turn to the door, and reached out to touch his arm, her glance once more becoming grave, worried. "Jeff, Noah can't have done something really bad, can he? Like —"

"You know him better than that," he cut in quickly, very positively, knowing how much she needed his reassurance. Even though he wasn't altogether certain of what he was about to say he told her, "He acted to me like someone had thrown a bad scare into him. But you know and I know he'd never do anything really wrong."

"You believe that?"

"I do."

Over the next five minutes, after she had watched Kindred drive off in the buckboard and then gone back to her room to get her coat, Cathy was finding a hesitant relief in what he had said. There was solid consolation in knowing that Jeff Kindred still had faith in Noah.

She left the store and had barely come onto the walk when a glance along the darkened street showed her the lighted window over Harmer's store obliquely across the way. And as she crossed the street, knowing Codrick must be in his office, she was trying to think of what to tell him. She had a strong pride, and for some inexplicable reason found herself rebelling at the thought of discussing Noah's difficulties with him.

It struck her then that her outlook had subtly changed overnight. Last night she had gone to Codrick's house wanting his help. Yet tonight, with even more reason to worry, her intuition told her to keep her troubles to herself as far as he was concerned. It was all at once unsettling to realize that in just one day Jeff Kindred had become the one and only person she relied on.

Two days ago Kindred had been nothing more than her partner in business, a man who had held himself strangely apart from any but the necessary personal contacts with her. Yet now he had become a real friend, someone she knew well and felt strongly attracted to.

By the time she had climbed the stairway and was knocking on Codrick's door she had thought out what she was to say to him. She would show none of her concern, would talk to him straightforwardly about the possibility of getting his client to buy only a part of Ladder.

Codrick appeared unaccountably on edge as he opened the door. But then as he saw who it was his easy smile came, and he said cordially, "Now isn't this a nice surprise. Come in, Cathy."

He took her hand as she entered, his expression turning quizzical as he caught her seriousness. "Something's happened," he said.

"Nothing too bad, Hugh."

He closed the door, motioning to an upholstered chair at the wall near his desk. But she was quick to say, "I won't stay. This will take only a minute." Pausing, she saw that it wouldn't be necessary to more than mention Noah to him. And she went on, "Hugh, we've decided to talk to that man about his offer. At least —"

The momentary look of outright delight that crossed his handsome face made her break off her words, hardly believing his reaction. "You seem glad," she said in amazement. "Why?"

His confusion then was obvious. "Glad? No, not glad at all," he said in an attempt to cover his betrayal of his feelings. Then he was adding in his usual suave way, "Or perhaps I am glad, Cathy. If you have to let the place go, this means I've got you the most for it anyone will pay."

"I was about to tell you that we've decided to take the offer on only part of Ladder."

"Part of it?" He frowned. "I don't understand."

"Noah has decided to sell his share. Kindred and I wonder if your man would want to buy just that much."

He shook his head. "Not a chance, Cathy. He'd want all or nothing." He eyed her narrowly then, asking, "What happened to Noah?"

"I can't tell exactly. Because . . . well, because I really don't know," she said lamely. "But he wants to sell his share. It seems a good chance of our being ahead of the bank for once."

"He's in trouble?"

She found herself resenting his curiosity and bridled, "Did I say he was?"

"I shouldn't be asking," he stated humbly, seeing he had gone too far. Then, with a shake of the head, he told her, "My man just wouldn't be interested in such a proposition."

Her depression was gripping her once more as she said, "Hugh, I'd like to go to this man and talk to him. Who is he?"

"Can't tell you. His name wasn't to be brought into it."

"But can't you see how much this means to us?" She disliked having to plead with him, but nevertheless went on, "If I could only talk to him I might persuade him."

He shook his head, saying nothing, and she was all at once really angry. "Hugh, this isn't like you. What possible harm would there be in my knowing who he is?"

Her tone brought color to his face. She didn't understand his manner then as he dropped his glance and turned away, striding slowly across to the desk, then facing around again.

"What harm would there be?" she insisted.

All at once, very deliberately, he was saying, "All right. Since you've put it that way

I will tell you." He hesitated. And when he next spoke it was the gravest tone she had ever heard him use. "Cathy, I'm the one who wants to buy Ladder."

Shock and disbelief held her speechless. He hurried on, "I've saved some money. Not enough, but enough so the bank will go along with me on this. I've made an offer that's better than fair. You were in trouble. This seemed a good way of helping."

Now she had forgotten that faint feeling of antagonism toward him as she breathed, "Hugh, that's one of the most generous things I've ever heard of. But . . . but you're a lawyer. You couldn't . . . you know nothing of ranching."

"You haven't heard the rest of it." Once again his glance refused to meet hers. "I'd decided you'd lose Ladder in the end. That didn't seem right. You belong there, rather than slaving in that damned store." He was obviously embarrassed now as he looked directly at her. "Cathy, I'd hoped that Ladder would be my wedding gift to you."

She was incredulous, bewildered. She stammered, "Hugh, I . . . This is something I hadn't —"

He lifted a hand to silence her. "You're not to decide now. And you're not to think of Ladder when you do decide. But it's there, yours, if you'll take me along with it."

Unexpectedly coming across to the door then, he opened it and stepped aside. His move startled her. At the same time she was ashamed at feeling a real relief at the prospect of leaving.

She came to the door, then hesitated, trying to think of something to tell him. He must have sensed how awkward this moment was for her, for he smiled wryly, saying, "I'd hoped you'd learn this a different way, Cathy, but now that you know I'm glad it's over with."

She said the only thing that occurred to her. "Thank you, Hugh," and went out onto the landing.

She was trembling, still bewildered, as she took the steps downward.

Shortly before Cathy left the lawyer's office, Jeff Kindred reached a forks in the road a quarter of a mile beyond the lower edge of town and reined his team into the left hand track, leaving the main one that skirted the foothills and climbed to the pass by a more circuitous route.

This road he was taking had been little used since the mines had played out. Parts of it were rough, a few places were washed out. But it was open, and it touched the lower edge of Ladder's meadow before angling south and losing itself in the scattering of abandoned mines cluttering the peak country to the south of the pass.

The buckboard had gone two hundred yards beyond the forks when the sound of a horse coming up from behind intruded upon Kindred's somber preoccupation. He looked around, making out the vague shape of a rider approaching. Then shortly he was mistrusting what he saw.

Seconds later he knew from the markings of the paint horse back there that this could be no one but Noah. And he drew rein, turning on the seat as the buckboard rolled to a stop.

Noah came in alongside the front wheel of Kindred's side. For a moment they regarded each other silently. Then Noah said almost casually, "Goin' the wrong way, aren't you?"

"Taking some things up to the meadow for Ordway. The sheepman." Kindred showed his strong surprise then as he drawled, "Thought you'd be twenty miles from here by now."

The starlight let him make out Noah's crooked smile. Then his partner was saying,

"So did I. But I'd spotted you on the way in and got to thinkin' what a damned ornery trick I pulled on you and Cathy. So I waited out here, hopin' to catch you on the way home."

He stepped out of the saddle now and without explanation walked on back to tie his reins to one of the end-gate braces. Then, rounding the rig to the far side, he climbed up alongside Kindred, drawling, "I've got some things to say. You might as well be on your way while you listen."

Puzzled, half-angry, Kindred slapped the team with reins and the buckboard rolled on. For long seconds Noah sat without speaking. Then all at once he was saying, "I've given you a rough time. I'd cut my heart out and hand it across if it'd make up for things."

"What's done's done," Kindred said quietly. "We can't forget that. But what you're doing now is something else again. Start runnin' from this thing, whatever it is, and you'll likely get the habit."

"Don't think I don't know that," Noah said brittlely. "But you'll see why it has to be." He sighed heavily, continuing, "I've had a hell of a week, the worst ever."

With a baffled shake of the head, he began telling of having ridden up to Duval's store along the pass road one night a week ago, of starting to drink. At this point Kindred interrupted him, saying tonelessly, "The last time you came back from Frenchy's I went up there and told him if he ever gave you another drink I'd be back and tear his place apart. I'll do it, too."

"Don't blame Frenchy," Noah said. "He wasn't going to —"

"I blame him and he'll answer for this," Kindred cut in. "Why do you always pick his place? He's shady, so is everyone that hangs out up there."

Noah smiled ruefully. "So they are. But they don't talk. Any place else I'd go the whole damn' country would know I was raisin' hell." He sighed heavily, shortly continuing. "Anyway, that poison got to me. Once it had, I couldn't quit. Along about the third or fourth day I ran into this bird Reno. Know him?"

Kindred nodded. "Big. Rides a dun horse with a neck blaze."

"That's him. There are a couple more things you could know about him. He traps wolves and lives off the bounties. And I heard somewhere he's had a few close shaves with the law. They say he kicks around with some of the boys they've thought were swingin' the sticky loop."

"You pick good company," Kindred inserted dryly.

Noah ignored the remark. "Well, what got me into trouble was the cards. Me, Reno, Frenchy and some man by the name of Dooley got into a game."

Kindred drawled, "Now I'll really go have a talk with Frenchy."

Noah had been too intent on what he was saying to give Kindred's remark more than a passing notice, and he went on to tell of the game, of losing to Reno. He could remember that much but no more. He ended the recounting of Reno's story of how they came to be in the cabin on the far slope by saying in a hushed voice, "Me, a rustler!"

Kindred was too dumbfounded to find words just then, and for more than a minute he sat there bleakly considering what his partner had just told him, the staccato hoof-clop of the team seeming to pound home the sense of helplessness that was gripping him.

Then finally Noah was speaking once more. "So there you have it. But here's one more thing. On the way across here this morning I came by way of the meadow. Who should I run into up there in the timber near the fence but Ralph Blake. He told me about the sheep, about the slide. But he told me something else. It's hard to believe."

"Couldn't be any harder to believe than the rest of it."

"In a way it is," Noah said. "It was just a small thing he let slip. Remember how I said Reno had told me we drove those cattle up Dead Horse?"

At Kindred's nod, he went on, "Ralph was cussin' the sheep, the storm, everything. He just happened to mention that he and two of his sidekicks had been camped up Dead Horse night before last, the night Reno said we came up the canyon. Olds had sent them up there to beat the brush for what steers they could find."

Kindred looked around sharply. "How could that be?"

"You tell me. There's only one way up Dead Horse."

Kindred sat thinking of this contradiction, watching the dark shadows of the pines slip by as the team trotted down a slight incline. If he had been confused a minute ago by what Noah had told him, he was even more confused now. At length, with a grunt of irritation, he drawled, "Your friend Reno doesn't know the country."

"That's just it. He knows it like the back of his hand."

They sat wordless for a long interval, each

engrossed in his bleak thoughts, until finally Noah said, "There you have it. If I stay on, Ben Olds sooner or later misses his critters and starts snoopin'. If he ever ties me in with the thing, think how it'd be for Cathy."

"Think how it is for her now," Kindred said in a grating voice. "I saw her tonight. It's like you'd kicked her in the face."

"Better this way than her seein' me strung up for a rustler."

Kindred thought a moment. "Suppose you do leave, and suppose Olds finds out what happens. He'll still tag you with the thing even though you aren't around. Then where will that leave Cathy?"

"You're to tell her about this, Jeff. Tell her the next time you see her."

"Her knowing won't help any when the word gets out."

Noah lifted his hands helplessly, let them fall again. And for several minutes as the road dipped and climbed across the dark, timbered hills, he and Kindred didn't speak.

At length, Kindred broke the long silence between them. "There's one other thing you can do, Kid," he said gently. "Go to the law and own up to what you've done. Or go to Sorrell and tell him, offer to make good on it."

"He'd like nothing better than to see me

111

locked up," Noah countered. "Hell, didn't he always hate my old man for moving up there next to him years ago when he thought that graze was his?"

"Then I'd rather see you keep it quiet and stay on," Kindred insisted. "I'd back you to the limit if you wound up in trouble."

The argument went on, interrupted by long periods when neither spoke. In twenty more minutes the timber was thinning and Kindred could look ahead into the starlit distance and see the first open stretches of grass footing the broader sweep of the meadow.

Finally, using all the persuasion at his command, he drawled, "Let this thing lick you now and you're licked for good. Stick it out and you have a chance, your only chance. And if you can't stop thinking of yourself, think of Cathy too."

Noah remained wordless, and in several more minutes Kindred was leaving the grass-grown track, sending the team across the gently rolling sweep of meadow toward the dark shadow of Mirror Lake and the line of railroad grade in the upper distance.

When Noah finally did speak it was to ask gustily, "You know what you're saying, askin' me to stay on? We got our heads barely above water without this. Have Olds get next to this thing and we'd have to say good-bye to the outfit, everything."

Kindred could sense the uncertainty, the yielding, in his partner, and he said eagerly, "I'll run that chance."

"Then you and me'll have a little talk with our friend here about his sheep."

Excitement flared in Kindred at this indirect agreement of Noah's to remain on Ladder. He was deeply thankful, though he tried to make his tone casual as he asked, "What did you have in mind?"

"We won't rob him blind. But he does pay up something for the graze he's taking."

"He doesn't have anything to pay. He . . ." Kindred saw something that moment that made him break off his words. Shortly he was drawling, "Why the light, I wonder?"

Noah looked on ahead, seeing what had taken Kindred's attention. The line of boxcars showed indistinctly against the dark shadow of the mountain half a mile ahead. A light was glowing in the caboose window. And now as Kindred put the team to a faster trot, Noah asked, "Why not a light?"

"Pretty late for Ordway to be up, isn't it?"

"So it is."

They drove on, rapidly lessening the distance that separated them from the wrecked train. Then all at once Kindred was seeing something else, a thing that made him whip his animals with rein-ends and ask harshly, "What's wrong? The sheep're loose."

Small bunches of animals, barely visible in the darkness, were drifting off toward the north and away from the makeshift corral. In another few seconds his alarm heightened at seeing a figure running slowly away from the corral, and he pulled his team in that direction.

Fred Ordway heard the rattle of the buckboard and abruptly halted, swinging around and halfway lifting a rifle to his shoulder. He stayed that way until they came in on him. Then, recognizing Kindred, he stepped over to the rig, saying furiously:

"Look at the damned things, Jeff. They're headed straight for that fence! And here I am stranded afoot."

Kindred vaulted from the buckboard, at once going to his nearest animal and beginning to unbuckle its collar, saying crisply, "Take the other one, Fred. We'll head 'em off."

The next moment Noah was calling from behind the buckboard, "Which way?"

"Turn 'em back from the fence," Kindred answered, quickly stripping the harness from his animal.

Several seconds later, as Noah ran his paint horse off into the shadows, Ordway asked gruffly, "Who's he?"

"My partner." Kindred was tying the end of the long rein to the inside of his animal's bit. And the next moment as he went astride the horse he said urgently, "Make it fast, Fred."

He kicked the bay into a run, heading across to the line of the grade and then following it upward, wishing it was the buckskin mule he was riding. Shortly, leaving the embankment as it drew beyond the shoulder of the mountain, he caught a far glimpse of Noah angling away to his right, the paint still at a hard run.

He was overtaking small bunches of sheep drifting in the direction he was riding, the sight stirring a strong anger in him. And his thoughts were laden with a deep rancor as he tried to fathom what could lie behind this furtive, unfair molestation of Ordway. Yet his concern over the sheepman presently died as he peered off into the darkness, searching vainly for another glimpse of Noah, thinking back confusedly upon the things Noah had told him on the way up here.

The widely spaced posts of Wineglass's fence came suddenly in out of the obscurity ahead, and he had to draw rein sharply to keep the bay from running into the wire. He was walking the horse in on the nearest post with the hope that there was still time to turn the sheep back when all at once a pair of ewes trotted on past him and straight through the line of the wire.

Only then did he understand that the fence had been cut. And now his anger tightened into cold rage as he looked upon this further proof of someone having deliberately set about involving Ordway in trouble with Wineglass.

Gingerly putting the bay horse through the line of the fence, he held the animal to a slow walk, listening. An interval passed in which he caught no sound but the swish of the bay's hooves through the fetlock-deep grass. Then abruptly, very faintly, the rhythmic drumming of a running horse sounded in from the distance to his right. He at once turned in that direction, lifting the bay to a fast jog.

The hollow slam of a far-off gunshot suddenly exploded across the night. His nerves going tight, he quickly reached inside his coat to draw the .45 Colt from his belt, judging that the sound had come from straight ahead. And now he pushed the bay to a run for a good two hundred yards before stopping to listen once more.

He was sitting there stiffly, irritated at the heavy breathing of his animal, when a second explosion struck sharply out of the darkness ahead.

A strong apprehension gripped him as he bent low, thumb on the hammer of the Colt, and trotted the bay on down a gentle slope, warily studying the darkness. Some ten seconds later he made out what appeared to be a small black outcropping showing against the paler sweep of the meadow obliquely to his right. He paid it but scant attention, his glance still roving the furthest shadows.

He could see no moving thing, could hear nothing over the gentle whisper of his animals' hooves sliding through the grass. His wary glance swung slowly through a broad arc, at length coming around to the black marking on the meadow he had seen some seconds ago.

It was closer now, almost abreast him. He gave it a cursory inspection, his glance went beyond it. Then suddenly he was looking at it once again from a slightly different angle.

What he saw this second time made him wheel his animal sharply toward the spot. In three more seconds he jumped aground and ran across to kneel beside a sprawled shape.

For a moment sight of the dark stain on Noah Horn's shirt front held him rigid with fear. Then, reaching down, he felt of Noah's limp wrist.

A feeling of dread, of desperation, settled through him as his fingers tried vainly to catch the beat of Noah's pulse. And as the seconds ran on his deep affection for this man roused a panic in him, so that finally he tore his friend's shirt open and put his hand to the blood-smeared chest.

That moment a shout sounded faintly from above. He had been unwittingly holding his breath, and now he let it go in a lusty, angry hail, having recognized Ordway's voice as the one that had called. Then suddenly he was trembling in relief at feeling the faint pound of Noah's heart against his palm.

He moved quickly then, using Noah's shirt to wipe away the blood, breathing, "Kid, you're comin' around. Hear me?" knowing he had spoken more to bolster his hopes than in any belief that Noah could hear him.

He saw the white skin punctured low along his friend's ribs near the left center of the chest, the sight sending a knifing of fear through him. He hastily made a wad of the shirt tail and used Noah's belt to bind the cloth to the wound. He was tightening the belt when Ordway called again, the voice sounding much closer.

He shouted stridently, "Here! Hurry it!" taking off his coat and spreading it across his friend's upper body.

Less than a minute later the sheepman trotted his horse in out of the further shadows, pulling to a halt close by. Staring incredulously at Noah a brief moment, he asked hollowly, "Dead?"

"Not quite. But it's going to be a close thing." Coming erect, Kindred tried to keep from showing the panic he was feeling as he quickly added, "I've got to get him down to town, Fred. One of us has to bring the rig across here."

"That'll be me. And I'll side you to town."

"What about the sheep?"

"The hell with them till mornin'!"

Ordway was turning his animal away as he spoke, and now Kindred said urgently, "Let's have your coat." Then, as the other was shrugging out of his denim jumper, Kindred ran across and snatched up the bay's rein, leading the animal back, saying as he handed Ordway the rein, "If you've got blankets, bring 'em."

The sheepman nodded, kicking his horse into motion. The bay was reluctant to be

119

led, and Kindred stepped in and hit him across the rump. Then as both animals broke into a slow run up the slope, he turned back and picked up Ordway's coat. A moment later he was spreading it over his own, tucking both garments in at Noah's sides.

He knelt beside his friend once more, bending low, and was reassured by the faint sound of Noah's steady breathing. Squatting back on his heels then, he was trying to check his impatience and his feeling of utter helplessness over this delay. It would take Fred Ordway at least a quarter of an hour to return with the buckboard, and he tried to shut away the thought that Noah might not be alive at the end of that long interval.

Over the next few minutes a fury tightened in him as he tried to guess who had shot Noah down. The most logical answer seemed to be that it was Sorrell's men who had resorted to this crude means of bringing on trouble for Fred Ordway. If such turned out to be the case, he understood that he was indirectly to blame for this, and now he felt an impotent regret at having defied Sorrell yesterday. But he was also certain if Wineglass was to blame he would bring Frank Sorrell to an accounting for it.

He was bleakly thinking of all this, sitting with shoulders hunched against the stinging cold, when a remote, barely audible sound carried in to him from above. Thinking Ordway must be coming back with the buckboard, he looked out across the starlit meadow, half rising.

Suddenly he was crouching again, reaching to his belt for the .45 at sight of two indistinct shapes drifting slowly toward him out of the obscurity. The Colt held ready, he eased forward until he was lying full length against Noah.

The shadows took on the forms of two riders, their outlines presently lying sharp against the paler sweep of grass. They were perhaps sixty yards away and walking their horses on a line that would take them obliquely past Kindred at a good distance when first one, then the other, halted to sit motionless for several seconds.

Abruptly Kindred saw one man turn and look at his companion. Then, quite plainly, he was hearing a deeptoned voice say, "What do you make of it, Ben?"

"You heard the shots, same as I did."

"Sure, but not the hollerin'."

"I'd lay my last dollar someone called from across here."

The interchange filled Kindred with a wary puzzlement. One of this pair was Ben Olds. He failed to recognize the other. But, more important was the implication that these Wineglass men were as ignorant as he of the circumstances behind the shooting.

For a moment he carefully weighed the possibility that they had seen him, had purposely set out to deceive him. But then as he remembered how closely he had come to riding straight on past Noah, at a much lesser distance than these two were from this spot now, he knew that they couldn't have recognized the dark pattern his shape and Noah's made against the ground. And he just as logically ruled out the possibility that one of these two had shot Noah. If one of them had, and if they had heard him shouting, they would be far from here by now.

The voice of the first man all at once cut across his confused thinking. "Hear anything, Ben?"

There was a long moment's silence. Then: "Sounds like a team and wagon."

Kindred saw both men turn in the direction of a sound he was hearing for the first time. He knew it must be Ordway bringing the buckboard down the meadow. A moment later Ben Olds was saying gruffly, "We better move," and the two men walked their animals away into the darkness to his right, away from the sound.

He was still lying there, eyeing the obscurity that had swallowed the pair, when Fred Ordway drove the buckboard on down to him some three minutes later.

"Still alive?" the sheepman at once asked.

Kindred nodded, still looking in the direction the Wineglass men had taken. And now Ordway came across and together they lifted Noah's limp weight. On the way across to the buckboard, the sheepman announced, "We'll put his head up beyond the seat. Helped myself to some of the cushions from the car. But the best I could do was one blanket. Think it'll be enough to keep him warm?"

Kindred had scarcely heard him and made no reply as he eyed the darkness off to his right. Then shortly Ordway was asking testily, "What's got into you?"

That instant Kindred caught a hint of movement against the obscurity off there. "We've got visitors, Fred," he said as he came in alongside the rig's wheel and lifted Noah's shoulders higher.

Ordway halted at once, and Kindred told him urgently, "Finish this and then stay set!"

Kindred could vaguely see the two Wineglass men now as they walked their horses in this direction. Lowering Noah's loose frame gently into the buckboard, he afterward crouched and swung in under the rig's bed close to the front wheel. A glance at Ordway showed him that the man had seen the two approaching riders and was reaching for the gun at his hip. "Forget that, Fred!" he said sharply. "Get the blanket on him. Let on like you haven't seen 'em. You're alone if they ask."

"Who is it?"

"Ben Olds and one of his men. Quiet now!"

Crouching there, relieved as Ordway came forward to pull something from the seat, Kindred wondered how much trust he could put in his hunch that the rig's shadowed bulk had made it hard for Olds and his companion to be exactly sure of what they had seen some moments ago.

Ordway stepped up onto the wheel-hub now and the springs creaked under his weight. And Kindred slowly drew the .45, staring out through the wheel-spokes as the men approached.

They were a scant twenty yards away when Ben Olds called, "You there! Stand quiet!"

The rig's springs creaked once more, Olds' voice coming again on the heel of the sound. "We don't aim to start nothin', whoever you are. But you're lookin' down

124

the bore of a forty-four."

He was holding a gun half raised as he brought his animal in on the buckboard. The other man had swung wide of him and was also approaching. In several more seconds Olds, then his companion, brought their horses to a stand close in to the rig.

Olds' glance had been on Ordway. Kindred saw him look into the bed of the buckboard now, and even this poor light showed him the astonishment that crossed Olds' narrow face. "Horn? How'd this happen?"

"You got the gall to ask that?" Ordway's voice was brittle.

Olds nodded curtly to his companion. "Tell him, Ralph. Tell him where we was when the shots came."

" 'Way up yonder," the other said. "A mile from here anyway. You don't hang this on us, mister."

"Then who cut him down? You're the birds that —"

"Hold it, Fred!" Kindred called loudly. "Sit, you two."

He was staring across his sights at Ben Olds as he spoke, and for an instant as Olds' head jerked around he thought the man's gun hand was dropping toward him.

Then Ordway was saying, "Go ahead, make your try! He'll blow you in two," with so much menace in his tone that Olds visibly stiffened, afterward dropping his Colt to the ground.

The sheepman vaulted from the rig then, stepping in on Ralph Blake and reaching up to jerk the man's gun roughly from the holster. And now Kindred eased out from under the buckboard alongside Olds, who looked down at him to say, "You got this thing figured wrong, Kindred. Me and Ralph had nothin' —"

"Let's move, Fred," Kindred cut in on him. "We can hear their story later. Ben, you're coming with us."

"Where to?"

"Town. To jail."

Less than an hour after the buckboard left the meadow, a sound at the alley door of Cathy's room behind the bakery roused her and she lay for a moment drowsily listening. Then a knock sounded against the panel and she called sleepily, "Yes?"

"It's Jeff, Catherine."

Kindred's voice brought her wide awake, and she left her bed quickly to grope in the darkness for her robe hanging over the back of a nearby chair. As she pulled on the robe she sensed that it must be very late, and she was trying to put down a strong feeling of alarm as she opened the door.

But then the sight of Jeff Kindred's tall shape standing there against the deep shadows somehow reassured her. She was about to speak when he quietly told her, "Catherine, Noah's been hurt. We've taken him to the doctor's. Thought you'd want to go down there with me."

"Hurt?" she breathed in alarm. "Hurt how?"

Briefly, quietly, Kindred began speaking. And in a few more seconds she was interrupting him to ask in bewilderment, "But who could have wanted to shoot him?"

"We're not sure. Ordway and I gathered in Ben Olds and Ralph Blake and brought 'em in. They're in jail now. Tell you about it on the way to Codrick's. You'd better get dressed."

"Is it . . . Does he have a chance?" she asked haltingly.

"A good one, the doctor says. Just don't worry."

"I'll hurry." She closed the door and crossed the room wanting to believe Kindred's words. Yet by the time she had dressed and put on her coat there was a stark conviction in her that made her say as she opened the door again, "Jeff, he's dying, isn't he?"

"Far from it." He took her arm, leading

her into the darkness along the alley, adding, "He's going to be all right."

"If you say that I'll try and believe it." Some of her fear was leaving her. "But how did Noah happen to be with you?"

He told her about meeting Noah, told her they had argued about Noah staying. He made no mention of Reno, or of what Reno had told Noah, thinking that if his partner was staying it was up to him to decide how much he was to tell his sister.

He finished by saying, "So it looks like he's staying with us after all," hoping that this word would divert her attention from her worry over Noah's condition.

She reached over and put a hand on his. "Really, Jeff? You think there's a chance he will?"

"Far as I could see he'd decided it." His awareness of this girl, of her closeness and of the trust she was putting in him, was heightening as he led her along the narrow passageway flanking the bakery. He told her of his ride to Sorrell's fence and of finding Noah, saying simply, "Probably hit his head when he fell. Got knocked out. He could come out of it with no more than a lump on his head and a sore rib."

"Dr. Codrick didn't think it was too serious?"

He shrugged, taking her arm once more as they came to the street and turned onto the walk. And he was feeling her arm pressing his hand gently as he told her, "You know Codrick. Never says one way or the other. He could have that chunk of lead out by now."

They walked on in silence, Kindred thankful for the darkness that hid his expression. He was really worried though his concern was brought on more by the strangeness of William Codrick's behavior some ten minutes ago than by any real conviction that Noah was dying.

He and Ordway had carried Noah straight in to the medico's office, when they had seen a lamp burning. They had found the old man asleep in the easy chair in the bay. But once they had stretched Noah out on the table it had taken them at least two minutes to rouse the doctor. And even after the man was on his feet he had seemed drugged with sleep, his eyes heavy-lidded, his speech thick, almost a mumbling.

Kindred had been no more able to understand that than he had Hugh Codrick's manner when the lawyer shortly came downstairs and into the office. Hugh had seemed to notice his father's condition at once and had brusquely asked Kindred and

Ordway to leave, suggesting that Fred go down the street and bring Maud Wilson back to help his father. Now, thinking back on that confused interval, Kindred was asking himself if William Codrick was capable of performing an operation as delicate as the one necessary to remove the bullet from Noah's chest.

He and Cathy had left the plank walk behind and were passing the first houses when the girl abruptly asked, "Did you see Hugh?"

Kindred nodded. "He was there. He sent Fred after Maud."

Cathy sighed. "Then everything they can do has been done."

They walked on in silence for several more seconds before Cathy unexpectedly announced, "Jeff, we're not letting Ladder go. Not to Hugh . . ." She hesitated unaccountably at the mention of the lawyer's name, then nervously added, "Not to Hugh's man or anyone else."

"You saw him tonight?"

"Yes. He . . . His man isn't interested in a part share."

"Thought that'd be the way it would turn out."

"Even if Noah can't help for a long time, now that this has happened, you and I can

130

make things work some way."

He was weighing that new quality of intimacy in her tone he had noticed once before tonight as she went on, "It wouldn't be the same, would it, someone else having even a part of Ladder?"

"Not for me, it wouldn't."

"Hugh was so strange tonight," she said musingly, "so sure of himself."

"Sure about what?"

"Nothing definite," she said hurriedly, her tone once again oddly edged with nervousness. Then, unexpectedly, she was asking, "Is it wrong of me not to be quite sure of Hugh, Jeff?"

"Sure of him how?"

It was a long moment before she answered, "I can't explain. Some day I will, though."

He was puzzled by the strangeness of her words, and drawled, "I've got him pegged as the kind that decides on something and sets straight out after it. It must be he wouldn't —"

"You're mistaken there," she interrupted. "That would be your way, never his. It may be an unkind thing to say, but he goes around a thing, never straight at it." Her words were puzzling him more than ever as she laughed nervously, saying, "You can't be too interested in being my father confessor. Forgive me, Jeff. I . . . I'm trying to decide something that's no concern of yours. I'm talking nonsense."

"Not nonsense at all," Kindred told her. "You've got to get it thought out, whatever it is. As for Hugh, I envy him."

"Why should you?"

As her glance came around to him in genuine startlement, Kindred had no regret over having revealed so much of his thoughts. Though he hadn't been able to guess what was disturbing her — what lay behind her nervous manner — he nevertheless forgot that now and went on almost angrily, "At least give him credit for trying for the best there is."

There was a moment's silence. Then Cathy was murmuring surprisedly, "You may not know it, Jeff, but you've just said a very nice thing."

"Meant it." Glancing on along the street now to see the lighted window of William Codrick's office close ahead, Kindred added awkwardly, "They've pulled the shades. Must mean they've got to work."

Once again he could feel her arm tightening against the touch of his hand. And then she was saying, "Just being with you makes it easier. You make me feel that everything's going to come out right."

Hugh Codrick had been looking over his father's shoulder, watching the medico use the probe. A lightheadedness was bothering him now as it often did at the sight of blood, and he turned away.

The next moment the old man was saying in a slurred, weary tone, "Well, we can't wait for Maud. You'll have to help. Get your hands washed."

"He seems pretty low, dad. Has he a chance?"

"A good one, if I don't fail him." The doctor looked at his hands, his stare bleak as he saw their trembling. "Why did I have to dose myself tonight?" he burst out angrily. "If I'd only known."

"But you didn't know, so let's make the best of it."

"You'll have to keep an eye on me, Hugh."

His step lagging, the medico crossed to the work-shelf along the far wall to snuff the flame of an alcohol burner under a pan of instruments he had been boiling. He looked around at the lawyer then, abruptly frowning as he stared at him out of heavy-lidded eyes. "You're pale, Hugh. Now's no time to lose your nerve. You've seen worse than a hole in a man's chest."

Hugh nodded. "I'll be ready when you need me." He was standing before the washstand in the corner, and now he rolled his sleeves and filled a basin with water, asking, "Find the bullet?"

"Yes. It's against the pericardium. Bruised it. Going to be a tricky thing to get it out."

The lawyer nodded perfunctorily, scarcely thinking of Noah any longer as he remembered that Kindred had told him of having overheard Olds' and Blake's conversation up there on the meadow. It had been then, on learning that Kindred could rule out the most obvious men to blame for the shooting, that Codrick had become so apprehensive as to ask Kindred and Ordway to leave. A sullen anger was in him over his quirk of circumstance having increased the risk Reno had run in turning the sheep out, and now he was regretting having sent the man up there on such an errand as the conviction hardened in him that Reno, no one else, had shot Noah.

His thinking suddenly became panicked as he thought of the possibility of Noah living through this. For if Noah had recognized Reno as the man who had cut him down, and if Noah was ever able to tell Kindred who had done the shooting, then

Kindred would logically hunt Reno down and try and make him talk. If the big man ever did talk then he, Codrick, had lost everything.

A real panic was gripping him now as he heard the hall door open and close. He looked around at his father, who had turned and was watching the office door. When several more seconds had passed without the sound of steps coming along the hallway, the doctor shrugged, saying, "Can't be Maud," and went to the table to unfold a clean sheet and spread it over Noah's lower body.

"Ready?" the medico asked, looking around at his son.

Hugh nodded, coming across to stand at his father's elbow alongside a small table holding the pan of instruments. "Open that box of lint," the old man said, the thickness of his words jarring Hugh from his frightened preoccupation.

Eyeing the doctor closely now as he set to work, Hugh presently saw him blink, then shake his head as though to bring himself more fully awake. The hand that held the thin scalpel, usually so deft and sure, was trembling so uncontrollably that finally the medico rested his forearm against Noah's chest to steady it. The old man's thin face would now and then relax into an expression of vacancy, and he several times paused to lean heavily against the table's edge.

Nothing but William Codrick's strength of will was keeping him awake some two minutes later when he breathed in relief, "There. Now we have it. The small forceps, Hugh. Quickly!"

A wary glance over his father's shoulder brought Hugh's eyes wider open. He was standing very close behind his parent. And now, looking furtively down at the medico's elbow, he turned sharply away, hitting the elbow solidly with his hip.

He was reaching to the pan of instruments when the doctor groaned softly, and as softly cried, "No, Hugh! My God, no!"

Hugh looked around in feigned alarm. "What's wrong?"

"You hit . . ." The old man checked his words. His face was ashen, his eyes wore a stunned expression as he took in his son's blandly innocent look.

He glanced quickly down at his patient once more. With a feeble shake of the head, he said in a quavering voice, "He's dead."

"Dead?" Hugh's look was one of disbelief. He stepped closer, eyeing Noah. Then, with a deep sigh, he put an arm about his father's shoulders. "No one could have done more for him. No one."

William Codrick reached across to pull the sheet up over Noah's head, saying in a lost, halting voice, "I . . . I guess not, son."

# FOUR

Barely a minute after Hugh Codrick had come from the office to tell the four people who waited in the hallway of Noah's death, Fred Ordway softly closed the front door and followed Maud Wilson across the porch and down the steps. As they took the dirt path along the darkened street, the girl said musingly, "It was strange, wasn't it?"

He waited several seconds for her to add to what she had said, then asked, "What was?"

"The way Cathy turned to Jeff when Hugh told her. I would have expected it to be the other way around."

Ordway was a little annoyed at having to listen to something that didn't even remotely concern him. "What other way?"

"I'd thought she and Hugh were quite serious about each other."

Ordway paid her words only a slight attention. And now as he trudged on he forgot everything but his own troubles. He was feeling miserable, his thoughts tinged with a self-loathing.

He was so wholly absorbed by what he was contemplating that it presently startled him to hear the girl say, "It really wouldn't have made any difference if I'd been there a minute earlier. Even five minutes."

He shrugged. "More of my luck."

"But what if you did stop at the wrong house first? I could hear you through the window. I was up by the time you got to our place."

He drawled ruefully, "Miss, I've been poison to lot of people lately. Tonight is just more of the same."

"You shouldn't say that. Or even think it."

Grunting his disgust, Ordway walked on, and shortly the girl was asking, "You mean it's your fault the train was wrecked?"

"Just forget the whole thing," he said tonelessly.

"But doesn't it help you to talk things like this out?" Maud insisted gently. "It always helps me." When he didn't answer, she went on, "You're thinking you're to blame for what happened simply because the trouble was over the sheep. But something you can't know is that Noah Horn has been headed for this sort of thing for a long time. You just happened to be there."

"He was there because of me, wasn't he?"

Ordway burst out. "He was helpin' me when he was cut down, wasn't he?"

She was wordless before his anger. And Fred Ordway said miserably, "Why has everything gone wrong lately? Why's it going wrong now? Here I'm even trampin' on you and we hardly know each other."

"Go on and tramp if it helps," she told him, her tone unruffled, sincere.

"Nothin' helps, miss. I climbed to the wrong side of the fence when I gave up cattle and bought those damned sheep. I been a stray ever since."

"That couldn't be, or a man like Jeff Kindred wouldn't be your friend."

"Jeff was crowded into it. He'll be regrettin' it soon as he has the chance to think it over."

"It's foolish to say that. As foolish as it is to think it. As for your being a sheepman, that's neither here nor there if you thought you were right in becoming one."

"I did think I was right," Ordway flared. "They came cheap and I had the chance of gathering in enough extra to quit runnin' a two-bit outfit."

"Then you were right. Which is what I'm trying to say."

Suddenly this all struck Ordway as being ludicrous, his being here in a strange town arguing the rights and wrongs of his actions with a girl he had known scarcely half an hour. He laughed outright, too loudly, unnaturally. "How'd we get wound up on this anyway? Why don't we drop it? Let's hear about you for a change."

He thought she was smiling at him as she said, "Now you sound nicer." Over a moment's hesitation, she went on, "There's blessed little you could want to know about me. I work with Cathy in the bake shop and help the doctor three afternoons a week. That way, mother doesn't have to do housework for other people any longer."

"Your father gone?"

She nodded. And Ordway, watching her, realized all at once that he had so far tonight been too preoccupied, too worried to realize that he had been in the company of an uncommonly nice girl. There was a straightforwardness, a placidity, in this Maud Wilson's nature that seemed to quiet the confusion and the desperation in him.

It struck him now that it had been a long time since he had the good fortune to know a girl even as slightly as he knew this one. That thought roused the bitterness in him once more, and before he quite realized it he was saying, "Good thing it's dark. Couldn't do folks' opinion of you much good to be seen in company with me."

"That's a risk I'll gladly take any time," Maud retorted, her tone betraying a real anger. "The next time you're in town if you want."

Ordway was surprised, embarrassed, though her words unaccountably bolstered his damaged pride. "You really mean that?"

"Of course, or I shouldn't have said it. I say only the things I mean."

He let his breath go in a perplexed sigh. "Could be I've been lookin' at things a bit wrong. But when you're mixed up like this it's hard to see straight."

"Yes, it is."

They were approaching her house now, and Ordway was experiencing a contrary regret at the prospect of having to leave her with such a poor opinion of him. He had been nothing but uncomfortable in this girl's presence, had made her nothing but uncomfortable. Yet he had in a strange way enjoyed being with her. She had made him start looking at things differently, had given him a new hold on his self-respect. She had gone out of her way to be nice despite his foul humor.

So as they reached the path leading to her house he paused and took off his hat, seeing that her expression was quite grave as she looked up at him. "Sorry you had to be on the receivin' end of all my belly achin'," he said guiltily. "You should've told me to shut up."

"No, because then there wouldn't have been a next time," came her surprisingly direct words. "I have enough faith in my judgment to know you can be a gentleman. Next time you will be one."

She must have been able to see the contriteness that crossed his face then, for she quickly told him, "That didn't sound the way I meant it. You are a gentleman." She was as embarrassed and confused as he now as she held out her hand. "Good night."

He took her hand, smiling uneasily. "Hope there will be a next time, miss. Just to prove I'm not always this sour."

"I'll be looking forward to it."

She turned away, and he stood watching until she had disappeared into the porch shadows.

Jeff Kindred was at the restaurant below the hotel early the next morning. It wasn't yet light enough to do without the lamps, and his meal was set before him with an apology for the morning batch of coffee not being quite ready.

He had barely commenced eating when the deputy who had last night locked up

Olds and Blake hurried in off the street to tell him, "Mr. Sorrell's at the jail. Wants to see you there right away."

Kindred's glance dropped to his plate, lifted again. "Think he'd let me finish this?"

"Better not. He said right away."

"Now did he?" Kindred mused, nodding gravely. Then: "Go back and ask him."

"Ask him what?"

"If he'll let me finish my meal."

The deputy's face reddened. "See here," he began, but checked his words when he saw the look that came to Kindred's dark eyes. He said uncertainly then, "Don't blame me if he ties into you."

"I won't." Kindred resumed his eating.

The slam of the street door brought his glance casually around. He saw the deputy stalking the still-shadowed street, heading back for the courthouse. And the restaurant owner, who had been eyeing him in surprise and considerable respect, grinned broadly, saying, "Wish more people would lay it on the line like that with Sorrell," afterward setting about the toweling of his counter.

The curt, faintly disdainful attitude Kindred had shown the deputy was but a slight indication of his mood this morning. Forty minutes ago, on waking in his hotel room, he had found himself thinking differently than he had last night. There was still that deep and baffled hurt in him over the pointlessness of Noah's death. He could still feel the helpless, bitter rage that had hardened in him last night as he took in Cathy's stunned bewilderment when Hugh Codrick told her of what had happened in the doctor's office.

But something beyond all this had been in his thoughts this morning. Without having willed it, he had reached the decision that he was to kill a man. Only after having made the decision had he coolly and carefully weighed the implications to what he intended doing, finding it necessary to alter his conception of what authority a man could arbitrarily take upon himself. He had great respect for human life. Nonetheless, the brutal and wanton disregard for life the killer had shown last night labeled him in Kindred's eyes as a man who had forfeited every right to his own.

Once convinced of this, Kindred had thought out what he was to do with typical thoroughness. He would first go to the law for help. With so little to go on, the law would probably fail him. In that event, he would take matters into his own hands. From now on little else besides the tracking down of the man who had killed his partner

145

could occupy him. And there was an impatience in him to set about that task today, this morning, now.

His truculent mood hadn't lessened some ten minutes later when he left the restaurant and walked to the courthouse. The jail was on the ground floor. He went straight to the sheriff's office and was surprised at finding the deputy alone in the room.

The man must have noticed his surprise, for he at once nodded to the heavy plank door of the jail, which stood slightly ajar. "He's in there," he told Kindred. "And he's hoppin' mad."

With a spare shrug, Kindred unceremoniously announced, "You can turn those two loose. I've decided to drop the charges."

"You've what?" The deputy's jaw went slack.

Kindred ignored the query as the jail door abruptly swung wider open. The next moment Frank Sorrell appeared from behind it, halting at once as he saw Kindred. Sudden indignation brightened the look in his eyes, and he intoned in a brittle voice, "Kindred, you go through with this and I'll see you licked in court and footing the costs. Olds and Blake had no more to —"

"Tell him what I just told you," Kindred interrupted tonelessly, eyeing the deputy.

146

"He just said he was droppin' the charges, Mr. Sorrell. Said I was to turn Ben and Ralph loose."

Surprise held Sorrell mute a long moment. Then, a look of satisfaction coming to his bearded face, he asked in heavy sarcasm, "What changed your mind so all of a sudden?"

"I happen to know they didn't do the shooting."

Sorrell's eyes showed incredulity, then outright indignation. "Then why the devil did you bring them in?"

"Because Ordway had to help me bring Noah down. Because if we'd left those two up there they'd have shot up Ordway's sheep. That's why you had them there, wasn't it?"

When Sorrell maintained a dogged, angry silence, Kindred nodded toward the jail door, telling the deputy, "Get your keys. I want a word with Blake before he leaves. Alone."

He stepped on past Sorrell and into the jail, the feeble light from its small window showing him Blake and Olds standing beyond the grilled partition dividing the two cells.

Olds drawled dryly, "So you changed your mind. Good thing."

147

Kindred made no reply, stepping aside as the deputy came on to unlock the further cell's door. Olds was the first man out, and he gave Kindred a baleful look as he went on into the office. Ralph Blake was following when Kindred eased in front of him to block his way.

Blake stepped surprisedly back into the cell then as Kindred told the deputy, "Close the door on your way out."

A moment later, as the heavy jail door swung shut, Blake asked, "What's comin' off here?" eyeing Kindred warily.

"Nothing to worry about," was Kindred's answer. "You were camped up Dead Horse three nights ago in the rain. That right?"

Blake nodded suspiciously, whereupon Kindred put a second question. "Exactly where was it?"

With a puzzled frown, Blake replied, "First you tell me what you're gettin' at."

"I don't tell you a thing. It isn't too late to change my mind about tearing up that warrant."

"I didn't do a damned thing up there last night but —"

"Where were you camped up Dead Horse?" Kindred cut in.

With a nervous, baffled sigh, the Wineglass man told him, "Where we always camp

148

when we clear out that upper end. There where the cut narrows down. Where we throw up that brush fence every year to drive into. Hell, you been there and know where it is."

A small excitement was beginning to stir in Kindred. "You had a fire, Noah said."

"We did. A big one. It was wet and we figured a fire and our ropes would hold what critters we'd gathered between there and the brush till mornin'."

All at once Kindred was struck by the thought, *Reno couldn't have known about the brush or he'd have told Noah a different story.* He was fairly certain of something, though because he wanted to be absolutely sure of it he asked, "You built your fence that afternoon?"

"Built it a week, ten days ago. Before the storm. Who'd hold off on that big a job till the minute we needed it?"

"How solid was the fence?"

"Solid enough to keep those steers from breakin' through."

Over a slight pause, Kindred asked, "You didn't see anyone up there that night?"

"No one but my two partners, Len Small and Bill Hunker."

"Could someone have slipped past without your seeing them?"

Blake thought a moment, then shook his head emphatically. "Damned if they could've. A man couldn't even have climbed around. That rock to both sides is straight up. One or more of us was up the whole night, too. We'd have seen anything that moved."

Kindred nodded, stepping out of Blake's way now, drawling, "That's all, Ralph."

But the Wineglass man made no move to leave the cell. He eyed Kindred with a per- plexed frown a long moment before saying mildly, "You're tryin' to get at something. What is it?"

"I wish I knew," Kindred sighed.

"Got something to do with Noah cashin' in?"

"It could have."

Blake's look was tinged with unmistakable sympathy then as he drawled, "You and us've had our outs. But Noah was a pretty right gent. I'm sorry as hell it turned out for him the way it did."

"So are we all."

"That all I can help you with?"

"Right now it is. I may look you up later."

Blake came on past Kindred now, and Kindred stood leaning against the grating, taking in the full implication of what he had learned. It was very plain to him that Reno

150

and Noah hadn't themselves ridden up Dead Horse three nights ago, let alone pushed a bunch of cattle through the canyon past the Wineglass camp. That one trail Blake and his men had been camped on was the only way out the head of Dead Horse.

Now he was beginning to suspect that no cattle had been stolen, that Reno had invented the story he'd given Noah. But why he had done so was something Kindred couldn't begin to fathom.

A low mutter of voices and the abrupt closing of the office door shortly prodded him from his confused preoccupation. He paced slowly out of the jail and into the office to find the deputy sitting behind the desk and Frank Sorrell standing in front of it.

He had something further to discuss with the deputy, but preferred waiting until the man was alone to do it. So he went to the hall door now. He was about to open it when Sorrell said aloofly, grudgingly, "Kindred, extend my sympathies to Catherine if you will. Hattie is stopping by later on to see if there's anything she can do."

"Good of her," Kindred said, looking around.

"I'll try and attend the services this afternoon." When Kindred nodded meagerly, saying nothing, the man brusquely stated, "I've told Olds that the sheep are your look-out from now on."

Kindred was surprised. "Ordway'll be glad to hear that."

"Understand, he's not to let them get out of hand. And he's to haul them out of there soon as the trains are running again." His tone still holding that quality of aloofness, Sorrell added, "Whoever shot Noah was hoping I'd get the blame. You realize that, don't you?"

"It's a possibility," Kindred conceded.

"More than a possibility. It's a fact." Scowling, Sorrell asked then, "Any notion of who did the shooting?"

Kindred gave a spare lift of the shoulders. "Hardly any." He was sensing in that moment that Sorrell's way of looking at things had undergone some subtle change. The man's manner was still unbending, dictatorial, yet the very fact of his allowing himself to show this much interest in Ladder's affairs was in itself proof of that change.

Realizing this, Kindred decided that now might after all be a good time to say what he had decided to say to the deputy. Glancing at the law man, he asked, "By the way, what're you going to do about it?"

"Me?" The man lifted hands outward in

a gesture of helplessness. "What can I do? They got me tied down here till the sheriff gets back."

"And when will that be?"

"Sometime tomorrow, if they can reach him. But Orville's 'way to hell and gone somewheres off there toward Twin Peaks."

"Doing what?"

The man's face turned ruddier. "Him and the Dober boys was going to try and bring home a wagonload of elk and deer meat to sell."

Kindred sighed gustily. "So he's gone for we don't know how long. And you have to be here to keep the stove going."

"I do what they tell me." The deputy shifted nervously in the chair, his look defiant.

Now Kindred glanced briefly at Sorrell, then back to the other once more. "Either of you know a man callin' himself Reno?"

Sorrell shook his head. But the deputy's look became alert. "I ought to. We've tried enough times to pin something on him."

"Pin what?"

"Anything. He travels with some pretty shifty birds."

"Where does he hang out?"

"Last I knew he'd boarded himself up a room in Frenchy Duval's barn and was livin'

153

there real snug. There's a back door he can duck out of. The woods is real close, which suits his style."

"He's a friend of Duval's?"

"He is if you can say Frenchy has any friends."

Kindred reached for the knob of the door now, looking back at them. It appeared that he was on the point of saying something. But in the end he only gave them a nod and left the room.

His steps were sounding along the hallway when the deputy eyed Frank Sorrell to say thoughtfully, "That Reno now. He's big. Big as a house. But somethin' tells me he maybe ain't big enough."

Sorrell, unamused by the remark, left the office, went out onto the street and up along it to his house. He had left home earlier without breakfast, which he found waiting for him now. He answered Harriet's questions gruffly and in a preoccupied way, for he was already regretting having made the concessions he had to Kindred.

He did admit to them, however. And his sister, on hearing that he had ordered Olds to stop watching the sheep, said, "Good. That's more like it."

Her remark rubbed Sorrell the wrong way. "Don't think Kindred's got me buffaloed," he growled. "There are other ways of keeping him in line."

Harriet's eyes sparkled with anger. "You never learn, do you?" she asked. "You never give an inch, regardless of anything."

Sorrell made no comment, knowing from experience that he could never best his sister in this sort of an argument. He finished his meal as quickly as he could and left the house.

Five minutes later he was in the bank, in John Watson's office. He stayed there but briefly and on his way out stopped just short of the street door to light a cigar. He was blowing out the match when Hugh Codrick approached the door and, about to enter, saw him standing there and hesitated.

Sorrell motioned the lawyer on in, saying perfunctorily as Codrick entered, "Might as well have our talk here instead of later in the office." He added in a slightly warmer tone, "It's the devil of a shame about young Horn. You might tell Catherine how much I regret it."

"I will, Mr. Sorrell."

"Now about this confounded road," Sorrell said quickly. "How far have you gone with it?"

"About as far as I can till the hearing."

"Duval's finished dickering with those

neighbors of his on the right of way?"

Codrick nodded. "About. He's even paid out some money."

"How much?"

"Maybe a hundred. But we owe more. All he's laid out is option money."

Sorrell was standing with his back to the bank entrance. Now, hearing the door open, he stepped aside and looked around at the man who had come in, saying, " 'Morning, Martin," taking in Martin Semple's sober answering nod as the man came past him.

Though he didn't at all understand why the assayer had given Codrick an unmistakably nervous glance, he put that from mind now, telling the lawyer, "A hundred's not too much of a loss to take." He noticed Codrick's slight frown, and added, "Of course there'll be your fee."

Codrick laughed uneasily. "It won't be much. But this is pretty sudden, your changing your mind."

"It hasn't been changed yet," Sorrell stated. "But I don't want it to go any further till I'm sure one way or the other. I'd like to pay up what I owe, then let the thing hang fire."

"As you say, sir. Would you like me to pay Duval off?"

Sorrell was about to answer in the affirmative. But then he was remembering Kindred having questioned the deputy about Reno, remembering that this Reno, whom he had never heard of before, lived at Duval's. And because he suspected that the man somehow fitted into the enigma of Noah Horn's death, because he was very curious as to what lay behind Kindred's interest in him, he eyed Codrick speculatively for several seconds, trying to decide something.

On sudden impulse he said, "No. Think I'll go up there myself. Maybe this morning."

"It's going to be a bitter day," Codrick told him. "Looks like snow in those clouds."

"A little snow never hurt a man."

Sorrell reached out and opened the door, the lawyer's parting words, "Thanks, Mr. Sorrell," striking him as a somewhat inane thing to say.

But the next moment he was forgetting that as he saw his sister step unexpectedly out from the foot of the stairway leading to his office. She came straight across to him, her face set in cold anger.

"Frank, what have you been doing in there?"

157

Her blunt question took him by surprise. "Why . . . why, talking to Hugh Codrick," he replied uncertainly.

"I know that. But what were you doing before that?"

Sorrell straightened in indignation, his face taking on color. "See here," he blustered, "what I do is my own —"

"I want to know what you went in to see John Watson about," Harriet interrupted, adding, "I want to know why you went straight to see him after telling me there were other ways of keeping Kindred in line."

Frank Sorrell had from bitter experience learned how futile it was to attempt to deceive his sister. Yet he nevertheless tried to look surprised, hurt, as he told her, "Woman, you think of the damnedest things!"

Her glance narrowed, and she stepped past him, saying crisply, "Perhaps I'd better go ask John Watson about this."

Sorrell was at once imagining what she would say to the bank president. And because he didn't at all relish being humbled even this publicly, he reached out and caught her by the arm, saying, "Hold on, now."

When she had turned to face him once

more, he admitted grudgingly, "John did say something about that note he's carrying on Ladder."

"What did he say about it?"

He shrugged. "What he naturally would. That now it looks like he'd have to call the note."

"And what did you tell him?"

There was anger, and a touch of contempt in her glance now that made him bridle, "Good Lord, woman, what could I tell him? I don't do his thinking for him."

"You don't?" Harriet laughed scornfully. In a voice heavy with sarcasm, she said, "Then it's about time you did. Just begin doing his thinking on Kindred's note. Tell him Kindred's a good risk, as good as any you know. Tell him his bank's in business to collect interest on loans. Tell him you think it's right to extend that note for another six months. Or better, a year."

"A year?" he echoed incredulously, yet feebly. "Why, by that time —"

"By that time Kindred and Cathy will have paid the note off," Harriet stated.

She waited, gauging his indecision, her cool glance not flinching. And in another moment she was quietly saying, "I mean this, Frank. Either you do it or I will."

Sighing resignedly, saying not a word,

Frank Sorrell turned and left her, going back into the bank.

Two hours after Sorrell's second visit to the bank, Jeff Kindred was staring out the window of the Difficult's shack, vacantly eyeing the feathery, gentle fall of snow hazing the up-canyon view. He had been talking for nearly five minutes, his tone even, unruffled.

Not once had Grace Hill interrupted him. She had sat stunned, stiff-backed in the rocker alongside the oilcloth-covered table. There had been no change in her bewildered expression beyond an increasing flintiness in her eyes.

Kindred was telling her only of the trouble at the meadow last night, making no mention of Noah's prior difficulties. He had dismissed them with the mere mention of Noah's return, for out of respect for his partner's memory he was hoping that he, Cathy, and possibly Hugh Codrick, would be the only ones ever to know of those difficulties.

At length he finished, and as silence fell over the room he looked briefly down at the melting snow-prints his boots had tracked across the worn floor, his glance at length going to Grace.

She unashamedly reached up and wiped her eyes, afterward saying in a voice that broke with a quiet fury, "Jeff, you must find that man. It's a dreadful thing to say, but I want you to kill him."

"But which man?" Kindred countered.

She made no answer as she rose from the chair and went to the shack's back corner to take down two china cups from an open cupboard built of dynamite cases. She brought the cups across to the hogsback stove, filled them from a pot of coffee, and turned back to the table once more. Handing Kindred one of the steaming cups, she burst out, "Damn the snow! Why would it have to come along at the very time you needed the ground bare?"

"Probably makes no difference," he told her, revealing none of the bitter disappointment he had felt since his visit to the meadow an hour ago. "Whoever he was, he most likely rode right alongside the ropes and made his cuts without once setting foot aground. The sheep would have tramped out the tracks of his horse on their way out. He eased along with the sheep till he was in deep grass. From there on he had it cinched. He moved real easy so as not to waken Ordway, pushin' the sheep on north. Then he had grass again across there where he cut the fence. Even bare ground wouldn't have given us much to go on."

Grace sighed helplessly as she sat in the rocker once more. "Where did you find Noah's horse?"

"Blake found him, brought him across to Fred Ordway just as I got there. Fred'll use him from now on."

Kindred was sitting the wrong way around in a straight chair, his arms across its back, and now he took a swallow of coffee, grimacing slightly, drawling, "That isn't all Blake did. When he heard Fred was trying to move the sheep down all by himself today he offered to help him." He saw Grace's astonishment and added, "Forgot to tell you, but Frank Sorrell has come partway to his senses. The sheep are my lookout from now on, he says. So Fred can stop jumpin' every time he sees his shadow."

"What came over the man?"

"Sorrell?" Kindred shrugged. "No telling."

"They're moving the sheep down? Where to?"

"That twenty acres we've got fenced right there at the layout. Fred and Blake should have them there by late afternoon."

Grace sat wordless for a brief interval. "Frank Sorrell stepping down off his high horse!" she finally murmured in a wondering way. "It's hard to believe."

"It was hard for me to believe when I heard it. He even said he'd try and be at the funeral this afternoon." Kindred gave the old woman an uneasy glance. "You can suit yourself about coming to the services, Grace. But I thought you'd want to know in time."

"I'd never have forgiven you if you hadn't let me know. Of course I'll go. Poor Cathy. She must feel like the world's against her."

He shook his head. "No. You know her better than that."

"I do," Grace conceded. "She's being fine about it." Dispiritedly, she breathed, "Makes my own worries seem like nothing at all."

"Your worries?" Kindred smiled faintly. "Don't tell me you have 'em too."

"I do." Grace eyed him speculatively a long moment before adding, "Which reminds me. When you've got more time and less on your mind, there's something I'd like to talk over with you."

He had inserted his remark a moment ago in a half-joking way. Now, taking in the unexpected response he had prompted in her, he said, "We've got four hours before we're due in town. What's worrying you?"

"Another time," she replied. But then abruptly she changed her mind, saying, "All right, now's a good a time as any. Jeff, I may be onto something big here."

"Big?" He suddenly caught her meaning. "You mean in the mine here? Gold?"

She nodded. "Gold."

He was unable to keep from smiling. "Everyone who's ever hunted the yellow stuff imagines that at one time or another, Grace."

"This is no imagining. I've been at this too long not to know the real thing."

"Good." He was serious again. "Glad to hear it."

"I don't know whether to be glad or not." Her look took on a worried quality. "The way it's turning out, I almost wish I hadn't run across this high grade." Over a brief pause, she went on, "You probably haven't heard much about the boom days here. Mr. Hill thought our fortunes were made when we leased this from Catherine's father. But, what with one thing and another, we barely paid our way. Then Mr. Hill died, the pay dirt thinned out and this lease wasn't worth the paper it was written on. It hasn't been for years, as you know."

She sighed, shaking her head. "Two weeks ago, even two days ago, I had hopes of seeing Mr. Hill's dream come true. Just seeing it happen would be enough for me. The money wouldn't matter much any longer, except for meaning your lease was worth something."

When she hesitated, he said solemnly, "That's a nice thought, Grace. But what's made you lose hope?"

"I haven't lost it," she retorted almost defiantly. Then, uncertainly, she added, "It's just that . . . that I can't be sure of what I've run onto."

"Aren't there ways of finding out?"

"Of course there are. I've been trying." Her glance narrowed now, and she asked, "Do you happen to know a man in town by the name of Semple? Martin Semple?"

He frowned. "No. But wasn't the name brought up in that stage robbery trial last year?"

"It was. Martin's son, Tadd, was mixed up in that. Martin used to be an assayer. A good one. Honest as they come. He'll still run an assay for anyone that wants it, though he doesn't do much of anything these days. He's well off."

She paused, and he queried, "What about him?"

"I said he was honest. But lately I've begun to wonder." When she saw the question in his eyes, she went on, "Jeff, I've taken ore down to that man lately to be tested. Ore I know was good, better than good. He's given me a poor report on every batch."

She saw him about to interrupt and said hurriedly, "I know you're about to say I could be wrong. I'd thought of that. So yesterday, just to prove it one way or another, I salted a sackful of what I was sure was real high grade. Salted it just a little, with dust I'd washed out of the tailings down there by the creek last summer. I took it down to him and waited till he was finished with it."

"How did it come out?"

"Just a trace of gold, he said. Not enough to pay for freighting it to the railroad and shipping it out. And I put in enough to mean more than that."

Kindred's brows lifted in faint surprise. "Then the man's not to be trusted. Go to someone else."

"That's easier said than done. In this game you have to know your man before you dare trust him." Her look was one of deep concern now. "I keep asking myself what reason Martin Semple could have for trying to fool me. It can't be because he's out to make a grab for himself. He's got too much money to bother. So there's another reason."

"You'll probably never find out what it is."

"Damned if I won't!" the old woman burst out. Then, her ire quickly leaving her, she said, "So you see what I'm up against there. But you haven't heard it all."

"There's more?"

"There is. Jeff, someone's watching me up here."

Kindred straightened in surprise. "Watching you how?"

"He's been in the mine. He may even know where I'm working." She read his disbelief and nodded extravagantly. "I almost told you about it the other night, but you had other things to think about. It all began a week ago when I was hunting up the canyon and came across this man's horse tied in the brush. A big roman-nosed dun with . . ."

Noticing his incredulity, she asked, "What's come over you?"

"You say a dun horse?" At her nod, Kindred put another question, his words deliberate, toneless. "A dun with a neck blaze?"

"How could you know about the blaze?" she asked wonderingly. "Yes, this animal had one. You know who he belongs to?"

Kindred gave a spare nod. "I may. But go on."

"Jeff, if you know who this devil is, I want you to tell me. I've been carrying a gun ever since. Been sleeping with it under my pillow. I'll use it on him if I ever get the chance. Now who is he?"

"There's a man callin' himself Reno rides a dun," Kindred told her. "He hangs out up around Duval's."

She shook her head. "The name doesn't mean a thing."

"Tell me the rest," he said quietly.

"Well, this horse was tied near the mouth of an air shaft up there. At first I was worried, thinking of someone roaming around in there. Finally I figured this gent might've holed up in the shaft to get out of the weather, for it was raining. But then yesterday morning I spotted tracks. Man tracks 'way back there in the mine."

"Reno's a big man. Were these outsize?"

"They were. But what scared me was that he was barefoot."

Kindred's puzzled look prompted her to say, "Don't you understand? He'd shed his boots because he was following me and didn't want me to hear him. Boots make an awful racket underground."

"Where was it you came across his prints?"

Her look took on a momentary quality of nervousness. Then, with a shrug of her bony shoulders, she told him, "You might as well know now as later. His tracks were up on B level, near where I'm working. There's a good head of water pours into the end of the north gallery up there. It runs out along a fault and into the creek above here. His feet had left their marks in the mud where the water splashes back a ways."

Kindred waited for her to continue. When she didn't, he asked, "That's all you can tell me?"

"All except that I got out of there quick, got my shotgun and rode up the canyon to where I'd found the dun before. There he was again, tied at the same spot. I waited around an hour, but this joker didn't show up. So I came back and went on down to town as I'd planned."

Kindred sighed gustily. And when he hadn't spoken in several more seconds, Grace said, "Now it's your turn."

"My turn for what?"

"For talkin'. What about this Reno? You've sat there lookin' smart as a fox ever since I mentioned the dun."

He came up off the chair and, staring

vacantly out the window and up-canyon, took his pipe from pocket and clenched it between his teeth, drawing on it quietly as he turned from the window to pace the width of the shack. His dark eyes wore an enigmatic, chill look, and his face was set grimly, in a way that startled Grace.

But she said nothing, watching him closely. Then in several more seconds his glance was abruptly meeting hers, and he drawled, "You'll have to wait on the explanations, Grace. But I'm going up to pay a call on this Reno. Today. Right now."

"All the way to Duval's?" she asked in surprise. "But you have to be back down at the church by three."

He nodded soberly. "I'll be there if I can. But if I'm not, you're to tell Catherine I'm looking into something that has to do with Noah. Just tell her that, no more."

He stepped across to the door and lifted his heavy cowhide coat down from a nail on the wall, saying quietly, "Now if you'll take me up to where you saw the dun, I'll be on my way."

The light snow of early morning in the high country had begun by sweeping the steep slopes dotted with the abandoned shaft houses of mines some miles to the

170

south of Eagle pass. Fitfully, yet gently, the flurries had swirled on across the pass itself to blanket the railroad grade, Ladder's meadow and the broad reach of boulder field above. Finally they had thinned and died out along a broad basin between the two highest peaks to the north.

For nearly an hour's interval the air was clear as spring water, the dark and flat-layered cloud mass turning the light blue and cold so that each detail of pine forest and craggy mountain shoulder lay sharply etched to the eye. Then, almost imperceptibly, the cloud settled and became formless, shrouding all the up country in a dense grey haze, and it began snowing heavily, steadily, with no let up.

The hush that settled over the whitening forest was utterly peaceful and soothing, giving a ghostly quality to the flight of birds and the furtive movements of animals. Riding steadily, the hoof falls of the buckskin mule gradually quieting to a mere whisper, Jeff Kindred found that this dead silent interval was working a change in him. His thoughts had been knotted and bitter since last night. Now they were unaccountably running straight and clear.

By midday, when he reached the point where the trail broke out of the pines above

171

Duval's, the snow was coming down so heavily that a man couldn't see across the hundred yard stretch separating the store from its nearest neighbor. And Kindred, stopping the mule at the timber's edge, was thankful for this thickening weather that was hiding him from sight of curious eyes.

He had tried, and failed, to plan out what he was to do once he arrived here, though there were one or two obvious preliminaries he knew he must observe. One of these he accomplished now, taking off his heavy knee-length coat, rolling it and tying it behind his saddle. The chill struck through his denim jacket, though he paid that scant attention as he stared at the barely visible shape of Duval's establishment, and at the even more indistinct outline of the barn behind it.

Unbuttoning the jacket now, then deliberately removing the cotton work-glove from his right hand, pocketing it, he reined the buckskin to the left in a slow walk along the tree margin, nearing barn and corral. He was squinting against the occasional wayward snowflakes swirling in under hatbrim as he closely eyed the barn, and presently he drew in a slow sigh at the faint sight of smoke drifting lazily up from a chimney sticking out of the back slope of the roof.

There was no window at this side of the barn. But there was a head-high door below the chimney, and he was recalling the deputy's words about Reno's living quarters as he pulled the mule back toward the trees, halting when he was certain that his outline blended into the dark background of the timber. He was so positioned now that he could see the corral, though not close enough to be sure of the colors or markings of the four animals in the enclosure.

He decided not to risk a closer inspection in search of the dun, and he turned back to the trail, presently riding out from the pines on a direct approach to the store. Halfway to it, he was surprised on recognizing a big roan gelding tied to the porch rail, and at once asked himself what Frank Sorrell could be doing at this out of the way spot on such a day. He dismissed the suspicion that Sorrell might be linked to Duval in what had happened to Noah, though his strong curiosity over the man's presence here stayed with him as he dismounted and wasted no time in tying his animal.

A brief glance through the dusty window of the bar room showed him only two figures in there, Duval's behind the bar, Frank Sorrell's tilted back in a chair close to the stove beyond a table at the room's center. The weak light cast by a pair of lamps at either end of the plain pine counter made him consider the possibility that someone else might be standing back in the shadows, though he knew he had to chance that. Neither Duval nor Sorrell were looking this way, so he crossed the porch as soundlessly as he could.

The rattle of the door's latch brought Duval's head around. The man had been talking, but now as he recognized the figure coming through the doorway a blend of surprise and alarm froze his expression. Kindred caught that look as he pushed the door to, as his glance roved the room to show him that these two were its only occupants. Then Sorrell was looking around, an odd expression of satisfaction creeping into his glance as he saw who it was.

Sorrell was the first to speak, though Kindred's regard had gone to Duval and wasn't straying. "You look like you could stand a drink, Kindred. Let me buy," the man said with startling affability.

Still eyeing the store owner, whose look had turned pale and wary, Kindred drawled, "Later maybe." He came across to the end of the bar, stepped behind it. Duval backed slowly away then as he came toward him,

174

though a moment later his glance dropped away from the man.

Kindred stopped at the exact center of the counter, reached in under it and lifted out a double-barreled shotgun. The weapon was rusted, its stock badly cracked. Eyeing it, Kindred said seriously, "If this thing ever split it'd spike a man clear through the shoulder, Frenchy. You oughtn't to keep it around."

Opening the gun, he took out the two brass-cased loads and tossed them carelessly to the floor. Then, holding the weapon by its barrels, he brought it stock down hard against the counter's edge.

The stock split, its bottom half swinging at right angles to the sharp-pointed top, the two held together by a wedge of tough walnut fibers. The sound had made Duval jerk more erect, had brought Frank Sorrell up out of his chair with a look of sober surprise.

Kindred's patience was all at once at an end. Duval was afraid, more than afraid, for his pasty face had gone ashen. Laying the broken shotgun on the counter now, Kindred said, "Put your hands on the bar, Frenchy. Turn your back."

"Listen, Kindred. I . . ." Duval checked his words, afterward meekly doing as he had been ordered.

Kindred came in alongside the man and ran a hand around his waist. Then he slapped his vest front up along the arm holes, asking, "No hide-outs, Frenchy?"

"I never carry iron. You know that," Duval answered.

"Then get out there where I can keep an eye on you."

The store owner was edging hesitantly out from the bar's end when Kindred looked at Sorrell to ask, "Have you told him?"

"Told him what?" Sorrell's look betrayed the fact that he was reserving judgment on what he had just witnessed.

"About Noah."

Sorrell nodded, and now Duval at once said, "Kindred, I'm sorry as can be about —"

"Has he been outside, or has he spoken to anybody since you told him?" Kindred asked Sorrell, having paid not the slightest attention to what the store owner was saying.

Frank Sorrell shook his head, whereupon Kindred eyed Duval to say tonelessly, "Frenchy, Noah and I had a talk before he was shot. One of the things we talked about was where he'd been this past week." He waited out a brief interval, letting his words carry their weight before adding, "It seems you've a poor memory for what I said last time I was here."

Duval swallowed with difficulty, opened his mouth to speak. But he was unable to find his voice, and Kindred, sickened at sight of the man's cringing fear, drawled, "All right, we'll get down to cases later. Right now I'll have a word with your friend Reno." He nodded to the room's rear door. "Go call him."

"But he ain't around," Duval finally found the voice to say. "Went down —"

"Go call him."

What little starch remained in the store-man left him now, and he turned apathetically toward the door. He was halfway to it when Kindred said, "Wait."

As Duval stopped and turned, Kindred looked at Sorrell again. "I came up here for some fun, Sorrell. Why did you?"

Nodding toward Duval, Sorrell answered, "We had some business to transact. I owed him some money."

Kindred considered this, finding Sorrell's answer somewhat unsatisfactory. "You wouldn't say what your business was, would you?" he asked.

"No reason why I shouldn't. Duval's been buying up right of way options for me for that toll road. He's laid out some money.

177

Now that I may be giving up the idea, I came to pay what I owed him."

"You may be giving it up?" Kindred surprisedly took in Sorrell's nod. "Glad to hear it," he said. "If you're finished, maybe you ought to be leaving. This snow'll be a foot deep before you get home."

He was startled then at seeing Frank Sorrell give Duval a stony stare, at hearing him say, "I listened to the beginning of this this morning. I'd like to see how you wind it up. You say you're up here for some fun. Maybe I'll have some too."

Kindred's first impulse was to be annoyed. He wanted no one to interfere in whatever the next few minutes were to bring. On the other hand, the look Sorrell had just directed at Duval was clear proof of something he hadn't until now known. Sorrell disliked Duval. He probably wouldn't take sides in what was to come. And he might prove valuable later as a witness to something.

So now Kindred nodded sparely at the store owner. "Get going. Stay there in the door. And yell so he'll be sure and hear."

On the heel of his words, he reached up lazily and lifted the horn-handled .45 from his belt. Duval's eyes came wider open in fright. He turned and went very carefully to the door and opened it.

"Reno!" His voice broke hoarsely. But then he called in a steadier tone, "Want to see you. Come on in."

A faint answering shout came from the direction of the barn as Duval shut the door and took two hesitant steps toward the room's center. Then, seeing Kindred all at once come toward him, he backed away until he stumbled against the wall, saying in a quavering voice, "Honest to God, Reno's to blame for this! He'd of cut my windpipe if I'd ever let on to you Horn had been here. He's . . ."

He saw that Kindred was coming to the door, not toward him, that Kindred wasn't even listening, and he let his words trail off helplessly. A moment later Kindred eased in to the hinged side of the door and with a spare lift of the Colt motioned him away.

The store man had reached the side of the stove opposite Sorrell when the crunch of bootsoles against the snow sounded from the rear of the building. Then Kindred could hear Reno stomping the snow from his feet on the back stoop.

The door abruptly swung open, Reno's deep voice at the same time asking querulously, "Didn't I say I wanted sleep? Can't a man . . ." He evidently saw Sorrell then, for he came on in without finishing what he

179

had been about to say, his back turned to Kindred as he reached behind him to close the door.

Kindred hesitated perhaps a second, taken aback by this man's huge proportions. Reno stood almost a full head taller than he. The man's vast muscular strength was made obvious by a thick neck sloping into heavy shoulders and wide chest. Kindred judged that Reno must outweigh him by forty or more pounds.

But then he forgot all this as cold anger tightened in him. The next moment he reached out, lifted Reno's .44 from its thigh holster.

# FIVE

Feeling the weight of the .44 suddenly leave his thigh, Reno wheeled around, his big frame instinctively going into a half-crouch. Outright *startlement* showed in his eyes as he saw Kindred standing there.

Yet there was nothing menacing in Kindred's attitude. He held both guns at armlength at his sides, eyeing the big man steadily, almost impassively. And slowly the surprise left Reno's face, his look taking on a wary inscrutability as he backed away a step, asking:

"Who have we here, Frenchy?"

Duval answered tiredly, reluctantly, "Kindred."

Reno's eyes betrayed no surprise, convincing Kindred that he had asked the question only to gain time. And now, not wanting to give the man that time to think, Kindred drawled, "Tell him, Frenchy. Tell him about Noah."

"Horn's dead, Reno," Duval said meekly. "Somebody shot him last night."

The big man's brows lifted in a convincing

show of disbelief. "That so? Why tell me about it?"

Kindred said, "He died thinking he was a rustler, Reno."

"Now did he?" The other's tone was faintly amused. He wasn't afraid. Every added second was giving him a new hold on his ruffled confidence as he stated blandly, "I still want to know what this's got to do with me."

"Sorrell," Kindred said, "this man and Noah stole a bunch of your cattle three nights ago. Or Reno says they did. Noah didn't know what he was doing. Reno rodded the whole affair."

Looking past Reno, Kindred took in Frank Sorrell's outright amazement. He wanted to convince the man of what he was saying beyond all doubt, and added flatly, "They took these steers across the hills, where Reno sold them. Reno tried to split the payoff but Noah turned him down."

A brief silence hung on after he had spoken. Then Reno was saying, "Mr. Sorrell, this man's loco. He can't prove a word of what he's sayin' because there couldn't be any proof. Why isn't there? Cause what he says never happened. Let Olds go over your layout and see if one head is missin'."

"So my hunch was right," Kindred breathed.

Reno shook his head. "Don't know what your hunch was, neighbor. But you don't cinch no rustlin' on me."

"It was all a bluff then, what you told Noah?"

Once again Reno shook his head, this time with a baffled look. "Search me what you're talkin' about."

Kindred eased out from the wall, aware now that nothing could be accomplished by talk. Reno stood halfway between him and the stove, near a table and four chairs sitting against the wall. Kindred came past him now, keeping well out of arm-reach as he stopped in front of Sorrell. Still eyeing Reno, he said, "Sorrell, take these and keep Duval off my back." And he offered the man both guns.

Puzzled, looking at Kindred worriedly, Sorrell nevertheless took the weapons. "I'd be careful," he said.

A faint expression of eagerness crossed Reno's face now as Kindred deliberately stepped toward him. Kindred noticed that and disregarded it, the slowly tightening rage in him making him forget everything but the urge to beat this man senseless, or to maul him until the truth was forced out of him. Nothing but a mauling, or a bad beating, could accomplish that.

Reno's hands slowly lifted outward from his sides now. His arms bent slightly and he rocked forward on his toes. His stance was so plainly unlike that of a man who fights solely with his fists that Kindred was struck by the thought, *He'd break a man in two if he ever got a hold on him*. And suddenly Kindred knew how he was to fight.

He wasn't yet quite within reach of the big man when he all at once threw his left, swung knowing he was short of the mark. The next split-second Reno lunged fast at him, as Kindred had hoped he would, both arms lifting to the level of his waist but no further.

Kindred dodged quickly aside, then in again. He jabbed his right hard, his blow catching Reno on the neck rather than on the jaw, for the big man had seen his error and ducked. Lunging clear, Reno thrust out a boot, attempting to trip Kindred, not managing it.

In that scant second's space of time Kindred had learned two things. Reno was half bear, half cat, unbelievably quick. But he had a definite style of fighting, and only one. He would rather crush a man, break his back, than hit him. His fighting was of the kicking, kneeing, bone-breaking variety. Because he had probably never been seriously hurt by a blow, he scorned the use of his fists in favor of more effective ways of beating a man.

Caught too deliberately thinking this out, Kindred now barely managed to leap out of Reno's way as the big man lunged once more. For an instant Reno appeared off-balance, and Kindred again came at him from the side. He saw his error too late then as Reno turned nimbly and drove head-down for his knees.

He brought a knee up hard, aiming for the man's face, instead hitting shoulder with a drive that rolled Reno onto his side. Reno made a slashing reach with one arm as he went down, and the brute strength behind that forearm glancing off his thigh left Kindred's leg numb.

Reno rolled onto his feet in catlike quickness. He was crouching now, arms halfway extended. And in sudden fury at not having yet struck one telling blow, Kindred forgot all caution and came straight at the man. He drove in at those reaching arms, striking savagely at Reno's head and neck. The man crouched even lower. Kindred felt a knee connect solidly with Reno's face an instant before hig legs were swept from under him.

The next, he threw all his weight forward in a fall as Reno clamped a hold on his left leg.

They crashed to the floor with Reno's frame arching backward as he kept his hold. Kindred rolled hard to one side, trying to twist out of that grip. There were two seconds in which he thrashed wildly, Reno hanging onto his leg. Then Reno reached out with one arm in a quick but futile try at catching his other leg. And Kindred twisted free, his spur ripping open Reno's shirt and leaving a bloody gouge along the man's right cheek.

They came erect an instant later, Reno feinting another lunge, Kindred weaving away, the muscles of his left leg so badly wrenched that it almost buckled under him. He had learned his lesson on fighting this man on his own terms, and for several moments he coolly, carefully kept moving, always out of Reno's reach.

Finally Reno straightened, planted hands on hips. Blood was running down the line of his shelving jaw and dripping onto his chest. His breathing made a vast, heaving sound that filled the room as he growled, "Do you fight or don't —"

Kindred's fist smashing against his mouth cut off his words. Kindred had moved in fast, had thrown his right before Reno's arms could lift. And now he struck Reno's reaching left arm a choppy, hard blow that beat it down. Then boots planted solidly, he threw the weight of his upper body into a punch that caught Reno on the ear.

Reno stumbled sideward. Kindred hit him solidly once more, full in the face, hit him a lighter blow on the shoulder to keep him off balance. Reno pulled his head down and folded his arms across his face. The next moment his head snapped back and he was lifted more erect by a hard uppercut. Then Kindred was in close, beating the man's arms down, twice hitting him in the face.

Reno kicked out instinctively, using his only defense now. His boot smashed Kindred full on the knee. Kindred's leg gave way as the pain struck, and he fell forward, Reno's other knee catching him on the point of the chin. And for an instant Kindred's senses were numbed by blinding pain, and he was defenseless, falling full length.

Reno kicked savagely but groggily once more. His bootheel caught Kindred a glancing blow on cheekbone, and it was the searing burn of this blow, this new pain, that strangely steadied Kindred and instantly made him realize his danger.

He looked up to see Reno about to kick

him again. And instinctively he threw his frame in a frantic roll that carried him hard into the man's legs. He kept on rolling, feeling the floor shake as Reno fell heavily. Then he was slamming hard against the bar, hearing Frank Sorrell call in alarm, "Watch it!"

He looked around to see Reno charging him. Coming to hands and knees, he dove to one side, looking over his shoulder to see Reno crash into the long counter and wheel toward him. He heard bottles falling, smashing against the floor as the counter rocked back into place. He lunged erect. He was a split-second too late in wheeling out of Reno's way, and he struck out aimlessly with both hands as Reno closed on him. Then Reno's arms were clamped powerfully about his chest.

For an instant he was panicked. But then his fury and his hate for this man drove out the panic. And in a cold rage he arched his back powerfully against that hold. He elbowed the man's head, he lifted a knee hard into Reno's groin. With his other boot he smashed down on one of Reno's. And as Reno's hold suddenly weakened he struck the man's jaw with the heel of one hand, then with the other.

A savage, killing lust was in him now. He

didn't bother to step away as he hit Reno in the face. He saw the man's head tilt backward. He struck again, with a force that made his knuckles ache. He threw his other fist, Reno's bloody mouth his target. Now Reno staggered backward against the counter, arms spread wide, hands gripping the edge of the bar to hold himself upright.

Suddenly a look of feeble cunning came to Reno's eyes. Wheeling awkwardly, he snatched the shotgun from the counter. Kindred stood waiting as the man brought the gun down to the level of his waist and thumbed back both hammers.

The double click of the falling hammers laid a crisp, futile sound across the momentary silence. A look of desperation was in Reno's eyes. He brought the gun up and with an unsteady lunge at Kindred swung it club-fashion. Kindred took one spare step, nicely avoiding the shotgun's downswing.

He drew back his right arm as Reno wheeled on him and started lifting the weapon once more. He swung a blow that began at the level of his knees, putting all the drive of his tall frame behind it. He hit Reno solidly at the hinge of the jaw.

The man's massive body went suddenly loose. The shotgun clattered to the floor. A vacant stare was in Reno's eyes as he fell loosely forward.

Kindred caught him, taking a hold on his shirtfront to keep him from falling. Half turning, Kindred saw that the stove was eight feet away. Gathering all his strength, he heaved Reno's loose weight backward and squarely into the stove.

A jangle of iron rang through the room as the stove went over, spilling live coals across the floor. The stovepipe clattered down, billowing a cloud of soot. Sorrell and Duval backed quickly away as Reno moaned feebly and pulled one leg from contact with the stove's hot iron.

Tongues of flame suddenly licked upward from the base of the wall, the coals having ignited the resin in the bottom log. And Duval began pulling off his coat, frantically eyeing the flames. But then, giving Kindred a frightened glance, what he saw made him go motionless.

For the space of several seconds there was no sound in the room beyond the faint crackling of the flames. Frank Sorrell stared at Kindred, waiting as tensely as Duval was waiting. The store owner's look took on a real panic now as the flames mounted higher, reaching halfway up the tier of the tinder-dry logs.

Then, very quietly, Kindred was saying, "That was an accident, wasn't it, Sorrell?"

Sudden understanding crossed Sorrell's face. When he spoke it was in much the same tone as Kindred had used. "Looked like it to me."

"But my place'll burn down!"

Kindred nodded. "Everyone's going to be sayin' what a shame it was you were burned out, Frenchy. They'll say they didn't know you had it in you when they tell about how there might have been a chance of savin' some of your things if you hadn't thought so much of your friend here and dragged him out first thing. There'll be folks wanting to see you build a new store. No one's going to understand why you picked up and just left without so much as a word. Isn't that so, Sorrell?"

Frank Sorrell tilted his head in sober agreement. "Yes, that's probably the way it'll be."

Kindred's glance was fixed on Duval once more, taking in the man's lost, resigned look. "You got a wagon, Frenchy?" he asked.

He waited for the other's weak nod, then said, "Because I'll be wanting to take Reno on down to the sheriff. You might go look in his room for something to cover him with after you've got him loaded." Stepping back from the heat of the flames now, Kindred nodded down to Reno's sprawled shape. "Better hurry it before he fries."

Duval came forward with a lagging stride, his look dazed. He had to shield his face as he reached down, got a hold on his friend's boots, and dragged him toward the rear door.

That evening, just after six o'clock, as Hugh Codrick began sweeping the snow from the house walk, he was thinking that this had been a confusing day, yet on the whole a quite satisfactory one. The outcome of his talk with Sorrell this morning had been disappointing. But the possibility of his hopes being blighted for a fee on the toll road case had been outweighed by Cathy unexpectedly having looked to him this afternoon to attend to several of the important details at the church and cemetery.

He considered this sure sign of a yielding in Cathy as being far more important than the loss of a few dollars on a fee, though in reasoning this way he was trying not to listen to a mocking voice of conscience telling him that Jeff Kindred's strange absence from the services might possibly explain Cathy's having relied so heavily on him. Even so, he knew that the afternoon had brought him and Cathy closer to each other than at any time in the several years they had been friends. He believed firmly that it was only a matter of time until the girl would accept the offer he had made her last night.

Noah's untimely passing had brought no repercussions beyond those naturally to be expected. Word had reached the courthouse this afternoon that the sheriff would return day after tomorrow, though the several men Codrick had talked to today had little hope of the law accomplishing much in resolving the enigma of the shooting. The snow which had begun falling in the mountains early in the day, and in town during the burying this afternoon, had quieted the lawyer's worry over the possibility of Reno being tracked, though he was certain that the man had taken every precaution last night against this eventuality.

For the first time now Hugh Codrick was looking upon his chances of owning Ladder and the Difficult as being better than even. Noah was gone, the outfit was short-handed. Grace Hill must be utterly discouraged, possibly to the point of having given up hope entirely. Simply by sitting back and letting matters take their course, the outcome of events should be in his favor. Or so Codrick's reasoning ran.

He had spent some time today looking far ahead to that day when the Difficult would begin disgorging its thousands, perhaps its tens of thousands in gold. His getting the mine into operation would have to appear as though it had come about by accident, though he was leaving the details of this scheming until later, after he had accomplished the main objective. But in the end Grace Hill's lease would be canceled. He and Cathy would have more solid wealth than either of them would know what to do with.

When that day came, when he had started the several businesses he had in mind, Frank Sorrell would no longer be the most influential man in the country. And possibly, even probably, the name of Hugh Codrick would one day be respected as the Territory's voice in the United States Senate.

Only one thing, something Codrick looked upon as being almost insignificant, was even slightly troubling him at the moment. His father had returned from the funeral and immediately taken to his bed. Codrick had learned this from Maud Wilson, who had walked home from the church with the doctor and aferward stopped at the office to mention it on her way back to the bakery.

The medico, according to Maud, had been unusually quiet while they were together. He had no sooner set foot in the house than he had announced that it had been a trying day, that he was tired, that he needed rest. He had sent the word that Hugh wasn't to worry.

Nevertheless, Codrick had come straight on home along the dusk-shadowed street to find his parent sitting in bed reading a massive volume on internal medicine. The old man's appearance had mildly shocked his son. His face had been drawn and pale, his manner and tone lethargic, drained of what little animation he had shown during these past days. The afternoon had taken much out of him, and there wasn't much left to be taken.

Hugh had made it a point to be cheerful, and they had talked of nothing in particular. But at length William Codrick had unexpectedly and quietly asked, "Son, exactly what happened last night?"

The lawyer had tried to look puzzled. "When do you mean?"

"When I was working on Noah."

"Why, he simply gave out, didn't he?" had been Hugh's noncommittal answer.

"I'm asking you. Nothing was very clear at the time. It still isn't, though I haven't dosed myself once today."

"Seemed to me from the very first that he was too far gone, dad. From what little I know of such things no one can do anything about too much loss of blood. He was simply too weak to hold on."

The doctor had nodded soberly, tiredly. "That was my fear all along. But I also can't help thinking that perhaps I didn't do all I could've for him. I remember my hand slipping once, slipping badly."

These all-important words had brought a consoling smile to Hugh's face, and he had queried disarmingly, "How many times have you told me a man can never be a good doctor till he understands that dying is as inevitable as birth and stops worrying about it, dad?"

"Giving me some of my own medicine, are you?" William Codrick asked. He appeared relieved, and they had talked of other things.

Now, quite certain of having eased the doctor's sense of guilt over the apparent accident, Hugh Codrick was enjoying this mild exercise, enjoying the sight of the snow drifting so gently down to soften the lamplight glowing in the windows up along the dark street. The look of the street, its pines so unseasonably laden with heavy snow, made him think ahead to Christmas, and he was wondering if perhaps Cathy would give her answer before then, if they would be spending the day on Ladder. But this reminded him of the fact that Kindred still stood in the way of his realizing his ambition, and he was at once feeling letdown, dissatisfied.

He supposed that the most direct way of dealing with Kindred would be to tell the man flatly who wanted to buy Ladder and why, then to buy him out for whatever figure he set on his share. Perhaps Cathy had already told Kindred who had made the offer on the outfit. If so, Codrick judged him to be a man who would quietly step aside in a matter as delicate as this. If he didn't, then there might be ways of forcing him out, as Noah had been forced out.

At this point in his reasoning, Codrick knew he was in error. Last night he had been able to guess the underlying reason for Cathy's offering to sell Noah's share of Ladder. Noah's weakness had allowed him to be so thoroughly frightened that Codrick felt certain he would have left the country had he lived. Yet a far different approach would have to be made to the problem of forcing Kindred out if he refused to sell. The man had no weakness that Codrick was aware of. He was of a far different breed than Noah had been.

Codrick was thinking this, having nearly swept the walk clear, when he noticed a man coming along the near walk from the direction of the stores, a tall man. A moment later he was quite startled at recognizing Jeff Kindred's rangy shape, and as he nervously hurried the strokes of the broom he noticed that the man was limping, favoring his left leg, that his stride was awkward.

His curiosity over Kindred having walked this far down the street was answered several seconds later as Noah's partner neared the corner of the yard fence and called, "So here you are. Been looking all over town for you."

Codrick straightened, leaning on the broom. "Nothing the matter, is there?" he asked as Kindred halted in front of him.

"Not exactly. But I need some legal advice." When Kindred smiled, Codrick noticed that the left side of his face was swollen and bruised. Then Kindred was adding, "Advice I'll pay you for."

The lawyer ignored this last remark, dryly asking, "Is the other man in as bad shape as you?"

Kindred lifted a hand and gingerly felt of his cheek, his smile broadening. "For a wonder he's worse off."

"Who is he?"

"A man you probably don't know. Goes by the handle of Reno."

Codrick stiffened, unable to conceal his outright amazement. Realizing he had shown it, he quickly covered his confusion by asking, "Not the big gent who hangs out up around Duval's?"

"The same."

The lawyer felt it safe to show his incredulity. "And you've tangled with him? Licked him?"

"Had some luck, I guess," Kindred answered, at once continuing, "but what I want to see you about is that I've had him jailed on a rustling charge. I'd like you to tell me if I have a leg to stand on."

"Rustling?" Codrick echoed, a chill premonition settling through him. "What are your grounds for the charge?"

"He and Noah were mixed up in something a few nights ago when Noah was a little the worse for the bottle," Kindred replied readily enough. "Reno told him that they'd run off some Wineglass animals and got rid of them to some man over Gap way. He sold Noah such a convincing bill of

goods that the kid almost skipped the country, which is why Catherine offered you
Noah's share of the outfit last night. I
wanted to get the straight of it, so I went
up there to Duval's today to get the story
from Reno first hand."

Codrick waited for several seconds, getting a firm hold on his emotions before
querying, "And did you get it?"

"No. Didn't even begin to. Reno's never
heard of even a part of it. So I tried to beat
it out of him."

"Then did he talk?"

"Not a word."

The lawyer exhaled slowly and inaudibly
in relief, afterward saying, "From the sound
of it you don't have that leg to stand on."

"One more thing. Frank Sorrell happened
to be there and heard everything. He's
signed the warrant along with me. When he
heard I was coming down to talk it over
with you he said to ask if we could hold
Reno in jail till Olds has had time to look
things over."

This news of Frank Sorrell being a witness
to something he had never thought would
be known heightened the lawyer's confusion
and uncertainty now. Unable to think of an
answer to give Kindred, he said haltingly,
"You've raised a fine point there. I . . ."

Hesitating, he abruptly motioned toward the house. "Come on inside while I think this over. It's too cold to be out here unless a man's moving around." Not waiting for Kindred to say anything, he led the way up the walk, in several more seconds saying, "So this is why you didn't get to the funeral."

"I'm stopping to explain to Catherine soon as I leave here."

Once they were in the hallway, Codrick was still at a loss as to what he should say. The news Kindred had brought was so unsettling, possibly so dangerous for him, that he had to have time to think. And with a nod to one of the chairs, he told Kindred, "Have a seat, Jeff. My father's not so well tonight and I'd like to go up and see if there's anything he's needing."

"Go right ahead."

Codrick shrugged out of his coat, hung it on the mirrored stand by the door, and went to the stairs. His thoughts were angry now, resentful of Kindred's interference in a matter he had already dismissed from his mind. He saw that if Kindred and Sorrell pressed their charges Reno might sooner or later decide to talk and save his skin. If that happened, if Reno did talk, then Codrick was in real danger.

The lawyer's thoughts were in such turmoil that by the time he reached the head of the stairs he didn't dare risk letting his father see him. He went on back along the short upstairs hallway to his own room, went in and closed the door.

A minute later he had decided what he was to do, though giving Kindred legal advice on the matter was but a relatively unimportant preliminary. He left his room and went slowly back down the stairs, idly wondering why his father hadn't called to him.

His expression was severe as Kindred rose from the chair and eyed him questioningly. "Jeff," he began worriedly, "you've put yourself in a ticklish spot. Noah's word is all you've got on this?"

"Isn't that enough?"

"Ordinarily it would be. More than enough. But Noah can no longer testify. And hearsay isn't admissible in court as evidence."

"Hearsay?"

The lawyer nodded. "Yes. Your repeating what Noah told you would be ruled as hearsay. Unless," he added carefully, pointedly, "he told someone else his story. Cathy, for instance."

Kindred quickly shook his head. "He didn't tell her and she's not to know about this. Not ever, Codrick."

"As you say." Codrick shrugged. "So you see how you stand? Every word that Noah told you may be true. But where's our proof?"

Kindred stood soberly eyeing him. "What if Olds finds he's missin' some steers?"

"Then you'd have a case. One they could hang Reno on."

Kindred sighed resignedly. "All we can do is hope, then." He frowned thoughtfully then, adding, "There's one more thing I might be able to tie in. Let you know later what it is if I can work it out. Much obliged for the help."

He turned to the door, what he had said at once rousing an alarm in Codrick. And as he opened the door, the lawyer asked, "What's the thing you hope to tie him in on?"

"Rather not say right now. Not till I've seen a man first."

"Which man?"

Kindred smiled meagerly, shaking his head. "No use dragging him into this unless it's necessary."

Codrick was sullenly resenting the man's calm refusal to share this confidence. Yet he saw that any further insistence on his part would be unreasonable and might even rouse Kindred's suspicions. So he followed Kindred out onto the porch, saying as the man went down the steps, "If you see your man and get anything out of him, let me know. I'll be here all evening."

"Then you may see me."

Half an hour after Kindred had left Codrick's, Maud Wilson heard the street door of the bakery store open just as she was carrying a stack of counter trays from the work room. Coming from behind the curtain, seeing Fred Ordway standing there, she halted in pleased surprise.

He grinned broadly at sight of her. Then, noticing what she was carrying, he came on around the end of the counter, saying, "Let me give you a hand."

Maud was too flustered to remind him that this was one of the chores she did each night at closing time. She surrendered the trays, and he looked down at her to ask, "Where do they go?"

"Just set them there." She nodded to the counter directly in front of him.

All Ordway had to do was reach out and set the trays down. And suddenly they were both laughing, struck by the absurdity of his not even having had to move to carry her burden the remaining distance.

"Always glad to help a lady," Ordway told her as he went to the front of the counter once more, then leaned against it facing her.

He couldn't seem to stop smiling, nor could she, and after regarding him a moment she shook her head wonderingly and told him, "My, you are different tonight. What's happened?"

His glance bridled, though he couldn't hide his good spirits as he asked roughly, "Should anything've happened? You mean I'm acting like a gentleman for a change?"

"No, not that," Maud quickly answered. "But you're . . . well, just different."

He reached up to thumb his hat to the back of his head, drawling, "Fact is, I feel different. Real good, miss."

"Maud," she said.

"Maud then." His face reddened in pleasure. "Maud, I'm out of the woods."

She was pleased at discovering that this man had a lighthearted streak in him, in discovering that his smile was contagious and sincere. She was also pleased at finding that her judgment of him was being borne out, and now as she reached over to straighten the stack of trays she asked, "Out of the woods how?"

"We've moved the sheep down is how. Moved 'em while it was snowing today.

Now they're right there at Jeff's layout, all snug and inside a fence, with feed enough to carry 'em through."

"That's certainly cause to celebrate," Maud said, meaning it.

A shyness was in his glance then as he told her, "Celebratin' was what I had in mind. You know of anything we could do tonight; you and me together?" He took in her surprise and added, "It's Saturday. There ought to be something doing in this town."

Maud could scarcely believe what she was hearing. This Fred Ordway was a man who didn't mince words, and to realize that he had come straight to her with his good news was not only flattering but hard to believe. And it was with real regret that she had to tell him, "It wouldn't be proper, Fred. Not after what's happened to Cathy today."

"Guess it wouldn't," he agreed soberly. "How is she?"

"Better than this afternoon. Old Grace Hill was here at supper time. After she'd gone, Cathy seemed brighter, like she was thinking of something besides Noah. Then just a few minutes ago Jeff stopped in. I was in their way, but that didn't seem to matter. Just seeing him made her almost cheerful, even if she was so upset about his face being such a sight."

Ordway's jaw went slack. "What about his face?"

"Didn't you know? He was in a fight."

"The devil he was!"

Ordway's expression had taken on a concern that made Maud quickly tell him, "It's nothing to worry about. He's all right."

"But who'd he have the scrap with?"

"He wouldn't say, even to Cathy."

"Where is he now?"

She only shook her head, and after several moments Ordway's worried look thinned, the expression in his eyes resuming its animation of half a minute ago.

"Y' know what, Maud," he said abruptly, crossing his arms and leaning against the high, glass-fronted counter, "there's something I've wanted to talk over with Jeff. Something that came to me today. Had a lot of time to think on that drive down. Got to wondering if now wouldn't be as good a time as any to call it quits on the sheep. Sell 'em as soon as I can, then put the money into land. Land right here. This country may've been poison to me so far, but I like it and it'd start likin' me if I got me a small outfit and went back to cattle."

Maud carefully considered what he had

said as he eyed her closely. She felt the weight of his regard, wondering if she was mistaken in reading more into his words than he had intended. And shortly she was telling him, "A man could do worse. You could homestead up there to the north and save on having to spend for land."

"How's the country up there?"

"It's nice. Pretty. Having no road into it has been what's kept people out. But there's bound to be a road some day."

"Who cares about a road? We could . . ." He caught himself up short, his enthusiasm having almost led him into saying something he hadn't intended. And he hurried on, "A man back home made me an offer on my layout last year. The whole caboodle, sheep and all. He's still interested. So I was thinkin' to take a couple weeks and go back there and make a deal with him. Then I'd get back here this winter, build me some kind of a shelter, and start snakin' logs in so's next spring it wouldn't be any trouble at all to throw up a cabin."

Maud had closed the showcase and was now taking off her apron. She nodded her approval, hoping he wouldn't see how excited his words had made her.

He saw her lay the apron on the back counter, and he straightened, asking,

"You're through for the evenin'?"

"Yes. We usually close up a little after seven Saturdays."

His glance wavered a moment. Then he was looking at her again. "You're going home?" He waited for her nod. Then: "Mind if I walk along with you? It's a fine night. Makes you feel good just to be out in it, Maud, it's so quiet and peaceful."

She smiled at him. "Then wait while I go back and say goodnight to Cathy."

The night was quiet for Martin Semple, yet peace of mind was something he hadn't known for almost a year. The blight Tadd had put on his father's house had outwardly been forgotten months ago. Martin Semple and his wife, Ruth, went about their daily life much as though nothing had happened. If their son's near-disgrace had brought any change for them it lay in the fact of their feeling much closer to each other than before the trial.

Each was thankful, though for far different reasons, for Tadd's acquittal and his having left the country. Martin Semple had never once even remotely betrayed to the boy's mother his bitter knowledge of the new evidence against his son. Ordinarily he could endure the constant awareness of that knowledge throughout the day, for he could be with friends or otherwise busy himself so as to keep the matter thrust to the background of his mind. But the evenings were a different thing entirely.

Then, not being a drinking man — and either drink or cards being a man's chief excuse for not remaining at his fireside — Semple would sooner or later find himself alone with his thoughts. He had tried to interest Ruth in staying up beyond her usual hour, had tried to teach her cribbage, patience even. But her temperament was unsuited to concentrating on games, her thoughts were too flighty and uncalculating to offer her husband even fair opposition, so that she had wearied of trying to be amused by cards and had resumed her old habit of retiring as soon as the supper dishes were done and her sewing finished.

So, at a few minutes past eight tonight when someone knocked at the front door, Martin Semple was sitting alone in the parlor. He went to the door at once, turning up the lamp in the hall, welcoming this intrusion upon his bleak preoccupation.

When he saw who stood beyond the doorway it took him a moment to recall the man's name and say cordially, "Come in, won't you, Kindred?"

"Maybe I'd better not. If Mrs. Semple's

at home you'd probably rather we talked outside." Kindred saw that Semple was trying not to stare at the swollen side of his face. It was also plain that the man was quite puzzled, so he added, "What I wanted to see you about was Grace Hill."

"What about Mrs. Hill?" There was a guarded quality in the assayer's tone.

"Just a question or two about the tests you've run for her."

The way Semple's expression instantly froze, the shocked look that came to his eyes before he managed to veil his emotion, was painful to witness. Yet it was also clear proof to Kindred that Grace's suspicions were founded on something more solid than her imagining, and he crowded back a feeling of pity as he out-stared the man, who finally said, "If you'll wait I'll get my hat."

Semple left the door standing open as he turned and crossed to the foot of a stairway climbing out of the hall. "Ruth," he called, "I'm going down the street. There's a man here wants to talk with me."

"Then ask him in, Martin."

"He . . . we won't be gone long," Semple said lamely, glancing around at the doorway.

"Bundle up then. And put something on your feet."

"I will. Be back soon."

Semple stepped out of Kindred's line of vision then, shortly to reappear wearing overcoat and hat. He came out onto the porch, closed the door and said tonelessly, "A fine night to be out. Like Christmas."

Kindred purposely made no comment, wanting his silence to crowd the man, and they went on out to the street, Kindred favoring his left leg. Semple ignored the walk and kept straight on through the ankle-deep snow until they had reached the middle of the street.

Then, turning in the direction opposite the stores, he asked brittlely, "Now what about Mrs. Hill?"

"You can't guess?"

"I asked what about her." Semple's tone was sharp, irritated.

It was several seconds before Kindred spoke, "Semple, Grace has told me about the tests you've run for her. She's naturally disappointed in your reports."

"They speak for themselves," the assayer answered gruffly. "I can't find something that isn't there."

"We were wondering about that."

When Kindred didn't go on, Semple asked, "About what?"

"What she brought you yesterday, for one

thing. You see, she'd salted that ore with pure gold."

The assayer nervously cleared his throat. "Then perhaps I was in error."

"You were," Kindred agreed. "And it isn't the first time."

Semple all at once halted, facing Kindred, his look one of unmistakable outrage even though Kindred couldn't see his face too well in this poor light. "See here," the man said in a voice that trembled with emotion. "I have a reputation for honesty. Damned if you can say such a thing to me!"

"Can't I?" Kindred sensed that he could accomplish little by this approach to the question. He thought a moment, finally continuing in a quiet tone, "Semple, let me tell you of a thing or two before you get so red-headed. First, Grace has found a man watching her up there at the mine. A man they call Reno. Do you know him?"

Semple nodded curtly. "Know of him."

"Then you'll understand why Grace is worried. Why I'm looking into this for her. Now —"

"You'd better look somewhere else," Semple cut in angrily. "If someone is up there bothering the woman, let her take her troubles to the sheriff."

"There's more you don't know." Kin-

213

dred's tone was unruffled. "Reno being up there snooping around might not mean anything if we didn't know he'd been tangled up with Noah Horn in something."

Semple's manner lost its truculence. "With young Horn? Tangled up how?"

Kindred was on the point of explaining. But then he checked himself, trying to think of a way of impressing Semple, of perhaps frightening the man, without having to reveal the details of Noah's association with Reno. He saw no reason why he should be telling the assayer something he wasn't telling anyone, not even Cathy. And now he thought of another way of approaching this, and asked, "Noah's dead, isn't he?"

"You mean . . ."

As the other's words trailed off uncertainly, Kindred went on, "Reno's in jail, Semple. I've had him arrested."

It was a long moment before the assayer said feebly, almost inaudibly, "I don't understand."

"Think, and you'll understand," Kindred countered evasively, putting as severe an edge to his tone as he could command. He went on unfeelingly now, "Everything's bound to tie in sooner or later. For one, your telling Grace Hill her test samples are worthless. For another, Reno prowling around up there watching her. Last of all, Noah Horn's in his grave for a reason I know damned well has to do with all this."

They had been standing there in the middle of the street facing each other during this interchange. Now Semple turned abruptly and started back down the street, seeming unaware of Kindred as he walked along with head down, as though staring at the light puffs of snow his boots were lifting. He plodded on, Kindred limping along beside him, until they were past his house, until Kindred began to wonder if the man was going to say anything further.

Then all at once the assayer surprised him by muttering, low-voiced, "Tell the rest. I want to know everything there is to know."

Kindred was unprepared for the words, having mentioned almost everything that had occurred to him to use as a pry for loosening the man's tongue. So now all he could think of was to set about driving home his argument. "Semple, it's plain for anyone to see," he began. "You're respected here, trusted by everyone. Yet Grace knows you've been lying to her. And I know it."

He sensed that Semple was about to interrupt, and put in hastily, "Wait'll I've spoken my piece before you bother calling me a liar again. I was about to say that there's only one thing could have forced you to run the chance you're running." Staring at the man, he bluntly asked, "Who's blackmailing you, Semple?"

The other's head jerked up. His face appeared drawn, haggard in this weak light. Yet over the next few seconds he didn't even open his mouth to protest the indictment Kindred had put upon him, so that finally Kindred used the last word of persuasion that occurred to him. "And who is it that's sent our friend Reno up there to watch old Grace?"

They were abreast the first lighted store windows now, and as they strode slowly along through the steadily falling snow, Semple still holding his stubborn silence, Kindred deliberately answered his own question. "Whoever Reno's working for must be the same man that persuaded you to trick Grace. You wouldn't be doing it on your own, she says, because you're well off. Besides which, you're honest. All right then, if you're not doing it for yourself, you're doing it for someone else. That someone's the same man who dragged Reno into this."

There was a long moment's silence in which the only sound against the night's stillness was the dry crunching of their boots against the feathery snow. Then Semple was asking in a tight voice, "What makes you think Reno isn't watching Mrs. Hill on his own?"

"Because there'd be no way of his knowing that Grace is onto something. Because you're the only man besides me that knows anything about the gold up there in the Difficult. Or I think you are."

Kindred paused a moment, then mused, "Another thing. Reno's not the kind to've thought this out. He'd play a thing for the short haul, not the long one. He hasn't the brains, he wouldn't have the chance to get himself wound up in anything so complicated as this."

The twisted semblance of a smile came to Semple's thin face. "Hasn't it occurred to you that I might've hired Reno to watch Mrs. Hill?"

"It has. But it doesn't add up. Unless . . ."

Kindred's words broke off in outright startlement as a new thought struck him. It was a thing he had so far overlooked, and as he was trying to think it out Semple queried, "Unless what?"

"Unless you're the man Hugh Codrick's been making this offer for on Ladder."

The assayer tiredly shook his head. "I'm not the man. But of course there's no reason why you should believe me."

"No, there isn't."

Kindred's patience suddenly deserted him now and he drawled flatly, "Semple, you looked guilty as a man can look back there when I first mentioned Grace. You're scared. You're guilty as hell of misleading Grace. Why bother denying —"

The muffled, hollow slam of a gunshot suddenly struck against the stillness, the sound coming from ahead. As the pound of the explosion faded up the street, Semple halted. "What could that be?"

"Don't know and it doesn't matter." Kindred was as aware as Semple of the shot probably meaning trouble, yet he sensed that he had finally managed to undermine the assayer's obstinacy, and he went on stubbornly, "One man's already dead because he got too far into this thing. Another's in jail because he was tied up with it, whatever it is. I'd think a long time if I were you before I got any deeper into it."

A shout sounded from below, coming either from the hotel or the courthouse, Kindred couldn't decide which. And Semple said worriedly, dispiritedly, "Trouble of some kind down there."

"Sounds as though there might be," Kindred agreed. "But let's think about this trouble right here. Your trouble. You've lined yourself up with murder. You've set out to cheat a woman. Add to that your working with one of the shadiest tramps in the country and it's hard to believe. You may be in deep now, but you'll be in deeper if you keep on. Just think it over. Look ahead and see where you're going to wind up. Ask yourself how long you'll be able to sleep nights."

Semple's face was set bleakly as he stared on along the snow-hazed street toward the lights of the hotel. He said miserably, all but inaudibly, "Give a man time to think, will you, Kindred?"

"Take all the time you want."

Martin Semple trudged on then, walking somewhat aimlessly, his steps dragging as though he was all at once almost too tired to walk. Kindred stayed alongside him not even trying to think of anything more to say. He had said enough. He had finally broken through this man's reserve. It was up to Semple now.

Kindred had been staring along the street, and suddenly now against the deep shadows ahead he made out several figures hurrying from the hotel in the direction of the courthouse. A foreboding instantly laid its hold on him. The next moment he was reaching out to take the assayer's arm, saying urgently, "Let's see what this is."

Men were running along the near walk as Kindred and Semple reached the street's edge. Then shortly Kindred let go the man's arm and ran on ahead. His feeling of alarm heightened to such a point that when he reached the courthouse door he unceremoniously shouldered a slower man out of the way in his impatience to get inside.

A group of eight or ten men were crowded before the door to the sheriff's office. Kindred pushed roughly in among them, saying sharply, "Out of the way there," shoving past those who didn't immediately make room for him. In another moment he was jammed sideways between a pair of men in the doorway, and he ungently elbowed one of these aside, stumbling into still another man ahead.

Now he could look over the heads of the crowd filling the office, could see Frank Sorrell and the deputy standing with their backs to the jail door. A moment later Frank Sorrell lifted a hand and shouted over the restive hum of excited voices, "Let's get the room cleared. On your way, you men!"

"Hell, give us a look at him," someone explained.

The deputy answered angrily, "You've

seen a dead man before. Beat it! Get movin'."

The men ahead of Kindred turned reluctantly and started moving to the door. Kindred pushed his way through the jam and was shortly clear of it. Sorrell saw him now, and with a frown turned to say something to the deputy.

Then, as Kindred came up to them, Sorrell tilted his head curtly to indicate the law man, saying, "He wants to know where you were when the shot was fired, Kindred."

"Someone got to Reno?" Kindred asked, ignoring the deputy's suspicious glance.

Sorrell nodded, grimly eyeing the men filing out into the hall. "Shot him through the side of the head. There isn't much left of . . ." Shrugging, he added gruffly, "Better not go in there unless you have a strong stomach."

# SIX

A cold rage hit Kindred as he took in the implications to what Frank Sorrell had just told him. Reno was dead. He would never talk now. A bullet had wiped out the one slender chance of ever learning why Noah had been framed, possibly why he had died.

As he bridled his fury, Kindred remembered Sorrell's words of a moment ago. They wanted to know where he had been when the shot was fired. As one of the only three men who had known Reno was in jail, he would logically be a suspect.

Eyeing the deputy now, noticing the suspicion in the man's glance, Kindred said tonelessly, "Martin Semple and I were coming along the street above here when it happened. Semple's outside somewhere if you want to check on me."

The deputy at once moved out from the jail door, saying uncertainly, "It ain't that I don't believe you. But you're the one that swore out the warrant. After all, he gave you that lump on the side of your face." And he crossed the room and went into the hall, Kindred hearing him call loudly, "Anyone seen Martin Semple?"

Kindred stood eyeing Sorrell, the bleak run of his thoughts mirrored on his lean face. And Sorrell, misreading his expression, said gruffly, "You needn't look at me that way. I was over in the hotel talking with Kemp."

Kindred nodded. "Wasn't thinking of that," he said. Then he asked, "Who besides you and me knew Reno was in here?"

"No one so far as I know, except our friend here." Sorrell nodded to the door, to the deputy coming back through it.

The deputy closed the door. "Semple says the same thing you did, Kindred," he said. He swore deliberately then, shaking his head in bafflement, adding, "One of the boys took a look out back for tracks. But a damn' bunch of kids had been out there standin' on each other's shoulders looking in through the window. Spoiled our chances."

"You found the window open?" Kindred asked.

At Sorrell's nod, he put another question, this one to the law man. "Who else knew about Reno being in here?"

"Just you two and me."

An unsettling, quite unbelievable conviction was hardening in Kindred now as the deputy went on, "Me, I was over at the Buckhorn for the usual Saturday night game with Neal and Banks and a couple others. I'd fed Reno his supper, fixed the stove and left a lantern on outside his cell. You could've knocked me over with a feather when they come and told me."

Kindred had scarcely heard the man speak as his bleak awareness of something grew steadily stronger. And now, an urgency rising in him, he turned across the room and went to the door.

Sorrell said, "You're on your way somewhere, Kindred. What've you thought of?"

"Tell you later," was Kindred's brief answer as he left the room.

He made his way through the crowd lingering in the hallway, his hard glance searching for a glimpse of Martin Semple. In several more seconds he was seeing the man standing to one side of the double doors leading to the street. The assayer stepped out to meet him as he approached, and Kindred told him, "Outside," leading the way through the doors and onto the street.

He waited until Semple had come in alongside him. Seeing that several men stood close by, he impatiently led the way on along the walk until he was past the corner of the building, hearing Semple coming along behind him. Then abruptly he stopped and faced around, curtly saying, "He killed Reno and he'll see that you wind up the same way, Semple. Now's no time to stand on your pride. What's he been holding over you?"

"You know who he is then?" Semple asked lifelessly.

"I do."

"Say who he is."

"Hugh Codrick."

Kindred heard the man sigh. He said, "Frank Sorrell and the sheriff's man were the only two besides me who knew Reno was in there. And Codrick. I went to Codrick to see if a warrant would stand." He hesitated, then said sharply, "Come on, man! Tell it!"

"It goes no further?"

"No."

"He . . . Codrick defended my boy Tadd in that trial," Semple said now in a tired, beaten tone. "He found new evidence after the trial, or claimed he did. I couldn't risk making him prove it."

Shaking his head wearily, the assayer continued, "I've . . . It's been a nightmare, Kindred. Seeing that woman being cheated and having my hands tied. I've tried to get

225

clear of it, but he wouldn't let me go. So now I'm a —"

"How did he find out about Grace?" Kindred cut in tonelessly.

"Several months ago she come to him to find out how she stood on her leases with you people and Mr. Sorrell. He must have thought it queer, since he and everyone else supposes Mrs. Hill is welcome to live at the Difficult without the formality of a lease."

"She is," Kindred said. "The place is hers as long as she lives if she wants to stay."

Semple nodded. "Codrick came to me. This was while we were still friendly, before I knew what a cold-blooded devil he could be. He asked me casually about Mrs. Hill. I admitted I'd run some assays for her lately, admitted some of them had turned out to be fairly good. Then's when he began his blackmail. I've had to tell him —"

"Never mind the rest," Kindred interrupted. He half turned from the man, about to start down the street, saying gently, "If anything happens to me, you're to go to Sorrell and tell him everything."

Semple tilted his lead, his look grave, "This is something the law should deal with, Kindred. You can't risk . . ."

The assayer checked his words. For Jeff

Kindred was striding away from him down the walk.

The quietness of the building after Maud Wilson and Fred Ordway had gone only heightened a persistent restlessness that had been in Cathy since early evening. Now that she was alone she realized how keyed up she had been throughout the day. Contrarily, instead of tiring her the past few difficult hours had stirred a nervous energy in her that made the prospect of trying to go to sleep an impossible one.

Finally she went on into the store's work room, built up the fire in the stove and started heating a pail of water. She cleaned the chimneys of all the lamps and trimmed the wicks. She scoured the zinc-topped work table, knowing all the while that Maud had already cleaned it, that the chore was unnecessary.

Some minutes later, as she was kneeling behind the front room counter washing its bottom shelf, she heard the shot explode far up the street. She paused in her work, listening, but then when she heard nothing more over the next several seconds her curiosity died.

She had been thinking of Grace Hill's visit before supper, and of her disappointment later in seeing Jeff so briefly and not being able to talk with him alone. She had been shocked by sight of his bruised and swollen face, and she hadn't at all understood his evasive explanation when she had asked about it. In the end she had had to be satisfied with his word that he would tell her everything later.

She was still thinking of Kindred when she took the pail on back to refill it. It all at once surprised her to realize that her thoughts of him had all day long been warm, buoyant. And because her nature was so straight-forward she deliberately set about searching her emotions, wanting to understand them.

No sooner had she begun that than she was discovering things about herself she had scarcely been aware of over these two hectic days. In this comparatively brief space of time her sense of values, her outlook, had undergone a subtle change. Some deeper understanding had first of all prompted her to change her attitude toward Noah, to accept his weakness for what it was, a habit that had taken too strong a hold on him for anyone to break. She was certain now that her thoughts of him would gradually come to ignore the stigma these past months had put upon him, that in the end she would remember only the fun-loving and gentle side of his nature.

But if her understanding of Noah had changed, so also had her attitude toward Jeff Kindred. This all-important fact stood strangely apart from everything else that had happened these past few days. A week ago Kindred had been hardly more than a good acquaintance, a man she liked and respected as she did many of her men. Yet since then certain indefinable qualities in his nature had roused a new awareness of him.

She supposed that the stand he had taken on the sheep had been the beginning of this heightened interest in him. His outfacing Frank Sorrell there in the boxcar had shown her that he possessed strict and stubborn principles she admired equally as much as she did his tenacity in defending them. Since then her instinct had made her unconsciously turn to him in her trouble. And in realizing how he had steadied her, how he had last night made her see that Noah's dying didn't mean the end of everything, she grasped a new and awesome fact.

The knowledge came suddenly and in all its finality. One moment she was in complete ignorance of it. The next she knew with no shadow of a doubt that she loved Jeff Kindred.

A warm glow was in her. She was all at once trembling in the grip of a breathtaking excitement. A gladness rose from deep within her, and a longing for him.

She was standing there letting the blissful awareness of all this take its sure hold on her when a rattling of the front door intruded upon her thoughts. *It's Jeff,* she told herself. And she hurried to take off her apron and smooth her dress before she went into the front room.

Sight of Hugh Codrick standing beyond the window, hands held deep in the pockets of his heavy buffalo coat, at once dampened her good spirits. Crossing the room to the door she found herself almost resenting the prospect of having to talk with the lawyer just now. She wanted to think of nothing but Kindred. She wanted to be alone, to recall the little things about him that had so suddenly and startlingly come to mean so much to her. There was his tone of voice, the responsiveness of his glance, the easy, sure way he carried himself.

She was drawing the bolt on the door before she noticed the utterly grave set of Codrick's face. It reminded her of Kindred's seriousness last night as they had talked here before he left for the meadow.

Then she was opening the door, forcing

herself not to think of Kindred any longer as she said, "You look awfully serious, Hugh. Will you come in?"

"I will, thanks."

He took off his hat and came on into the room, his look still serious. Wondering at this, she was about to close the door when the sound of voices from up-street caught her attention. She listened a moment, heard someone shout and another man answer excitedly. She knew at once that something unusual was taking place, and turned to Codrick to ask, "What's happened up there?"

He unceremoniously reached across to push the door shut, telling her, "Sounded like a shot from somewhere above just as I was leaving the house. But let's forget it." He eyed her bleakly a moment, then bluntly announced, "Cathy, he's gone."

"Gone?" She couldn't understand. "Who?"

"My father."

"Oh, Hugh. No!" She was shocked, incredulous, and reached out to grip his arm, breathing, "The poor man."

He turned and laid his hat on the counter, saying quietly, "It's hard to get used to the idea even if I did know it was bound to happen any day. I . . ." He smiled feebly,

231

guiltily almost. "You were the only one I could come to, Cathy. As though you didn't have enough to think about."

"You should have come to me," she replied, at once made uneasy over the meaning he might read into her words.

"Then I'm glad I did." He unbuttoned his coat, continuing, "He was tired when he got back home this afternoon. Went right to bed. By the time I got there he seemed perfectly all right. No more tired than he is sometimes. We talked a while. He was almost cheerful, nothing wrong with him that I could see."

"Don't talk about it, Hugh," Cathy said gently.

"But I want to. It helps, if you don't mind."

"Of course I don't mind. But it's over now. It does no good to keep thinking about it."

"Jeff had been to see me along about six o'clock," he told her, disregarding what she had said and giving her an odd, probing glance. "Everything was quiet upstairs after he left. So I went on back to the kitchen and started warming up the supper Maud made us. When things were ready I went up and looked into his room. He was asleep, or so I thought. Just lying there with his watch in his hand, as though he'd looked to see what time it was and had decided to take a nap before we ate."

Cathy nodded, saying nothing. And shortly Codrick was telling her in a tight voice, "I came back down and read for maybe an hour. Put the food in the oven. Then just now, since it was getting so late; I went up to wake him. He was gone."

When she was sure he had finished, Cathy said softly, "I'm so glad it happened that way. He deserved a peaceful end."

Codrick drew in a breath and let it go in a sigh of resignation. "So it's over. I'm on my own. And a damned lonesome feeling it is."

The inference she put to his words made her nervous, made her avoid his glance and hastily ask, "Would you like a cup of coffee, Hugh? There was a cake left we could have along with it."

"No, nothing for me, thanks." He appeared unsure of himself then as he asked, "I'll have to let somebody know about this. But who? Dad was coroner."

"You could go to Frank Sorrell. Or why not Pete Ballew? He'd see to everything."

"Perhaps Pete would be best."

He reached for his hat and stood a moment looking at her, a slow, wistful smile coming to his face. Then suddenly he was saying, "Cathy, this means I'm sure of Ladder. Financially, I mean. Dad was always too busy to spend the money he took in. So I suppose you'd say I'm to be comfortably well off."

She could think of nothing to say in her uneasy awareness of what he was leading up to, so she merely nodded.

He stepped closer to her now and took her hand. "Do you see how much easier it makes it for us? Debts can bring plenty of misery. We still may have our troubles, but owing money won't be one of them."

She tried to smile but couldn't. "Hugh, I . . . I've been thinking about all this," she said haltingly. "There's something you should —"

His quick shake of the head silenced her. "Not now, Cathy," he told her. "Let's wait to talk about it. I want it to be right. It wasn't right last night and I regret that. But the next time we bring it up let's not have anything interfering. This is something we'll always want to remember."

She felt her face go hot in embarrassment. "But I'm trying to tell you that —"

"I know," he cut in. "You're trying to cheer me up. But I'd rather wait for that. Cathy, my father was as fine as any man

I'll ever know. Tonight I'm not thinking of anything but him. Do you mind?"

She understood now that it would be unfair, even brutal, to say what she had been about to say. After all, she did like this man, though now she was wishing only that he would leave before he guessed what lay behind her confusion and embarrassment.

He went to the door, opened it, then turned to give her a parting smile. "In a few days everything'll be different for us, Cathy. Then we can forget all this and start thinking of ourselves."

The sound of the door closing brought Cathy a feeling of vast relief. For a moment she guiltily considered the disappointment she would soon be bringing this man. But then she forced herself to think of Jeff Kindred once more, and her uneasiness over Codrick was gradually forgotten, along with everything but the wonder of what she had discovered tonight.

Jeff Kindred was four doors above the bakery, walking toward it on his way from the courthouse, when he saw a man leave the building and start obliquely across the street away from him. A moment later he recognized Codrick and quickened his stride, angling out so as to overtake the lawyer before he reached the far walk.

But then the thought of something cooled the blaze of rage in him, and he slowed his steps, knowing that if he and Codrick were to meet before he had seen Cathy there was every likelihood of his regretting it to the end of his days. So he went on, hearing the lawyer's muffled steps sounding against the plank walk opposite as the man headed down the street.

In a few more seconds he was abreast the bakery window and looking in to see Cathy behind the counter, reaching up to turn down a bracket lamp on the wall. His knock made her face around in surprise. When she saw who it was she smiled gladly and hurried to the door.

"You must have known I was thinking of you, Jeff."

The warmth and gentleness of her tone wasn't lost on him. Yet he was so bleakly and wholly absorbed in considering what he had seen on the street that he put his strong awareness of this girl aside, though he sensed that his soberness brought a look of concern to her face as he asked, "Codrick was here just now?"

She nodded, and without giving her the chance to speak he put another question. "How long has he been here?"

"Five minutes. Perhaps a little longer." She eyed him closely, trying to guess what lay behind his seriousness then as she told him, "Jeff, Doctor Codrick passed away tonight. Hugh came straight here to tell me."

Kindred was stunned, for a moment, held speechless before this news. Yet then he was feeling a deep thankfulness at William Codrick having been spared the shame and humiliation that would otherwise have come to him. And it was in keen relief that he drawled, "Perhaps it's as well. He was too good a man to have to keep on suffering."

"Hugh says he died in his sleep." An odd look of shyness came to Cathy's glance then, and she said hesitantly, "Jeff, there's something I want to tell you about Hugh."

She hurried her words, as though impatient to be done with them. "I haven't told you what he and I talked about last night when I went to ask him about the man who'd made the offer."

Hesitating a moment, she went on in a tone that was almost defiant. "He's the one who made the offer. He wanted to buy Ladder and give it to me. Give it as a wedding present. He asked me to marry him."

A feeling of dread settled through Kindred. He tried to tell himself that some freak of circumstance, not unalterable fact pointed to Hugh Codrick as being guilty of the murder of Reno. And he avoided Cathy's eyes, afraid that she might guess his thoughts as he said, "You're going to, of course."

"Jeff, look at me."

His glance lifted, and she met it with one that was gentle, very grave. "No, Jeff. I'm not marrying him."

The disbelief and the delight that eased the stony look from his face made her add, "I like Hugh and respect him. But marriage calls for more than that."

She didn't know the reason for the quick return of his seriousness then, nor why he asked, "You're sure of this, Catherine? Very sure?"

"As sure as I am of anything." She eyed him questioningly. "Something's worrying you, Jeff. What is it?"

"Give me a minute to think," he said.

She waited for him to continue. When several seconds had passed and he hadn't spoken, she said, "Has it anything to do with what you didn't tell me earlier?"

He lifted a hand to the swollen side of his face, smiling bleakly, admitting, "It does." Over a moment's awkward hesitation, he went on. "Don't know how much Grace told you about why I wasn't here this afternoon. But when I saw her this morning she had a lot to say about a man who'd been prowling around up there at the mine watching her."

He was carefully thinking out what he was to tell her of Reno, wanting to avoid any mention of Noah, as he went on. "She'd spotted this man's tracks in the mine. And once she'd come across his horse tied up the canyon near a tunnel opening. From the way she described the animal I thought I knew who he belonged to. It needed looking into. So I went on up to Duval's, where this man hangs out. Brought him back down with me this evenin' and had him locked up. Which is why I got back too late to get to the church."

"I told you before that it doesn't matter," she said. "But you haven't told all that happened, have you?"

Giving a spare lift of his wide shoulders, he said, "We took a few swings at each other before I persuaded him."

She eyed him speculatively. "Who was this man?"

"Calls himself Reno." He all at once saw a way of sidestepping any further questions on her part concerning Reno, and bluntly announced, "He's dead now. Someone shot him there in the jail not fifteen minutes ago."

"Shot him?" She was amazed. "But . . . you mean he was killed because of . . . of something that had to do with his watching Grace?"

At his nod, a sudden look of understanding brightened her glance, and she breathed, "Why, I heard a shot. It must have been the one."

Kindred said nothing, wanting her to take in the full implication of what he had told her. The next moment she was asking, "What can it all mean? What sort of trouble was Grace in?" She noticed the impassiveness that veiled his look then and insisted, "There's something more you're not telling me."

"There is, Catherine. Five minutes ago I wouldn't have dared tell it. Now I can. Without it hurting you."

"Hurting me? What is there about all this that could possibly hurt me?"

"There was Codrick," he replied gently.

The bewilderment that came to her eyes made him say awkwardly, "You'll maybe have to help me fit it all together. But first of all there were only three men besides the man in the sheriff's office who knew Reno was in that jail. I was one, Frank Sorrell another, and Hugh Codrick the third. Now I know Sorrell —"

The catch of her breath cut across his words. "Jeff! You're trying to tell me Hugh is a killer?"

He quickly shook his head. "I'm not that sure. But there's a better than even chance he may be." He waited a moment for his indictment to have its effect, then went on, "Look at the facts, Catherine. It was dark when I brought Reno in. It's Saturday and the sheriff's office was the only room open in the whole building. I'd driven Reno up the back street in a wagon, gone in that way with him. Not a soul was around to see us. And Sorrell and I made the deputy swear he wouldn't tell anybody about Reno being there."

"How did it happen Sorrell was with you?"

"He was at Duval's when Reno and I had our set-to. He heard enough to want to help. We agreed we'd hold Reno over the week-end without anyone knowing about it."

He was trying to avoid any mention of the rustling, any remote chance of Cathy ever being able to connect Noah with Reno, though he sensed now that his half-evasive answer might leave her dissatisfied. But she evidently accepted it, for shortly she asked, "Then how could Hugh know this Reno was there?"

"Because afterward I went to see him to find out if Sorrell and I were within our rights holding the man on a trumped up charge." He paused a moment before continuing, "I was on the street with a man when the shot cut loose. Sorrell was in the hotel, the deputy at the Buckhorn sitting in at a game. We've all got witnesses."

Cathy's glance all at once showed surprise. "But how could Hugh have done it, Jeff? He told me he heard the shot as he was leaving the house on his way here."

Her words made Kindred unsure of himself. He eased a step to one side now, leaning on the counter, his elbow touching the stack of trays Maud had left there earlier. "Maybe he was and maybe he wasn't leaving his house," he drawled thoughtfully. "He could still be the one who used the gun on Reno. He could've hurried down here from the jail and told you what he did, knowing there was a slim chance of anyone ever doubting his word. Remember, his father had just died. Anyone would be inclined to believe him just out of sympathy."

She gave him a long, measuring regard, murmuring, "I'm trying to see it the way you do, Jeff. But give me time." Then over a moment's pause, she said, "You haven't yet mentioned a reason for his wanting to see Reno dead."

"He had one. Reno knew too much about him."

She was again puzzled. "Knew too much about what?"

"About his wanting Ladder."

"But how can that have anything to do with this other?"

"Let's begin at the beginning," Kindred told her. "Months ago Grace went to Codrick to ask how she stood on her lease with us. Codrick thought that was strange and set about finding out why she was even thinking of the lease any longer."

He hesitated, groping for a way of explaining further without bringing in Martin Semple's name. But if he wanted to spare the man in this it was also far more important that he should have Cathy's complete understanding.

So at length he drawled, "Don't ask how I know this because I haven't the right to tell. But shortly after Grace saw Codrick he learned there was a good chance of her being onto a real find up at the Difficult. Learned it by blackmailing a man that did work for Grace."

"Martin Semple?" Cathy at once asked.

Kindred tried to hide his startlement, querying in as bland a tone as he could command, "Semple? Who's he?"

"It doesn't matter," Cathy replied. "His was just the first name that occurred to me. But go on."

"Codrick kept close tabs on her through this man," Kindred continued with relief. "Meantime, he'd hired Reno to watch her, probably to make sure it was Ladder's lease, not Sorrell's, she was working. He —"

"Is she really onto something worthwhile, Jeff? Could it mean we may some day be collecting something on the lease?"

"Hadn't thought of that," Kindred said in surprise truthfully. Yet even this possibility failed to excite him now in face of the other somber things that filled his mind, and he said, "Whether it's anything worthwhile or not, Codrick was sure enough that it was to set out to get Ladder."

He saw the incredulity, the near indignation, that edged into her glance, and quickly put in, "Understand, Codrick was probably honest as a man can be in wanting to marry you. That alone would've given him everything a man could want. But that came later, after he'd tried to buy the outfit in that roundabout way."

He took in her hesitant nod of understanding, and went on, "Everything fit his

244

plan. The layout was short of money and had no prospect of any ready cash turning up. We'd lost all those steers last spring, which meant we couldn't ship much this fall. Codrick laid his bet on the partnership being on its last legs, or nearly so. Then's when he made his offer. It appeared to be a natural thing to do, close as he was to our troubles. He even made it look like he was trying to help us out."

"And all the while he was really doing exactly the opposite," Cathy murmured.

Kindred tilted his head soberly, not speaking for a long moment, wanting her to understand this as fully as he did. Then at length he was saying, "When he didn't make any headway with his offer, when we just plugged along hoping —"

"Not we, Jeff," she interrupted. "It was you. Noah would have sold in a minute if you'd let him. And I didn't know enough about it to be sure of which way was right."

He gestured sparely with a lift of the hand, waving the words aside. "No matter whose notion it was, it threw a hitch on Codrick's plans. Then's when he decided on taking the one sure way of getting the place."

Cathy nodded humbly, saying low-voiced, angrily, "And to think he's been so sure of me."

This was an awkward moment for her, and Kindred tried to ease it for her by drawling, "One more thing played right into his hands. My scrap with Frank Sorrell over the sheep. He even used that to crowd us."

"Used it how, Jeff?"

"By trying to stir up trouble between us and Wineglass. This is only a guess, but I'd bank on Reno being the man that turned those sheep out and cut the fence. Codrick had him do it."

Sudden comprehension came to her. "Then that means Reno shot Noah?"

"We may never know. It's only a guess. But at least we're sure Blake and Olds didn't do it. And I doubt that it was Codrick. You were with him for a time after I left town. He'd have had to do some tall riding to get up the mountain before Noah and I did. And it would have taken him some time to turn the sheep out."

She moved her head slowly in bewilderment. "I'm so confused, Jeff. It's all so hard to believe."

"It is," he agreed. "Just as hard to believe as Frank Sorrell climbing down off the high horse finally and helping me instead of tying into me the way Codrick was so sure he would."

"What came over the man?"

"Search me. But he backed me up there at Duval's today."

Her look showed she was thinking of something else now. And a moment later she asked, "Then Reno knew too much? Is that why you're sure it was Hugh who killed him?"

"That's one reason."

She stared at him thoughtfully. "You say there's another man who's been working with Hugh. Couldn't he be the one who shot Reno?"

"He could be, except that he was on the street with me when it happened."

The gravity of her look then showed unmistakably that she was finally convinced of the truth of what he had told her. "So Hugh is a murderer." Her eyes mirrored a real panic then. "If he had asked me a month ago it might have turned out differently, Jeff. I didn't feel the same about him then as I did even an hour ago. I . . . I really liked him."

Kindred drawled soberly, "Let's hope I'm right about this. There's nothing at all to back a lot of it."

"But you have to be right. I'm as sure of it as you are." Her words were hushed now, all but inaudible as she murmured, "I would never have known, would I? Even if he and

I had lived on Ladder I'd never have known."

"Let's not think of what might have been," he drawled. "It didn't happen, which is what matters."

They stood wordless a long moment, until finally Cathy asked, "Jeff, could all this have anything to do with Noah acting the way he did yesterday?"

The question caught him off guard. All he could think of to say was, "How could it?"

"We know something happened, something he wouldn't talk about."

"Whatever it was, Noah couldn't have known about this," he said deliberately.

He decided then that same day, after time had dulled her grief over Noah's dying, he would tell her exactly what had happened, tell her of his conviction that Codrick had been behind the deception Reno had used in tricking her brother. But now was no time to add further confusion to her thoughts, and he stated warily, "I didn't even know about this till tonight. All I had to go on was what Grace told me about the man up there at the Difficult."

He had told her everything he could tell her, and all at once he was feeling an impatience to leave here, to find Codrick and make the man talk so as to rid himself of these few remaining doubts. But he knew he must keep from betraying that impatience, and now he glanced idly out the window, watching the play of the snow as it swirled gently against the lamplight.

Suddenly, quietly, Cathy said, "You're going to see Hugh tonight, aren't you, Jeff?"

He looked quickly around at her, scarcely believing the fear he saw in her eyes. All at once he knew the meaning of that fear, knew beyond any doubt what lay in this girl's heart. And in his humble, awed awareness of it, he said quietly, "This has to be settled sooner or later, Catherine. Nothing's to be gained by putting it off."

"But couldn't . . . wouldn't they arrest him?"

"Not with what little we have to go on," he told her, adding, "You're not to worry."

She nodded, her emotion momentarily too strong to speak against. It was several seconds before she found the voice to say, "You must come back, Jeff. It would . . . nothing matters to me but that. Nothing."

They were on the verge of something that made them both completely unaware of anything but each other, so that the footsteps sounding plainly against the planks outside were approaching the door before Kindred heard them. His glance reluctantly swung away from Cathy. He saw Hugh Codrick pushing the door open.

The lawyer's hat and the shoulders of his coat were powdered with snow. He hesitated on the threshold, giving Kindred a brief nod before he looked at Cathy to say, "Just wanted you to know that Pete is taking care of everything, Cathy. So you were right about my being able to count on him."

"Come in and close the door, Codrick."

The cool edge to Kindred's quiet-spoken words brought a frown to the lawyer's face. Puzzled, he stepped on in and pushed the door shut. Then Kindred was saying, "Catherine's told me about your father. A blessing he could go just when he did, isn't it?"

"Is it?" Codrick's look took on a faintly truculent quality. "I suppose you could look at it that way."

He eyed Cathy again now, what he saw once more bringing that quality of puzzlement to his glance. "Is something wrong?" he asked her. "You don't look well."

"She's been telling me about the offer you made on Ladder last night," Kindred put in quickly, not wanting Cathy to say anything. Then, very deliberately, he added, "I've been telling her what's in back of it."

There was a convincing bewilderment in

the change of the lawyer's expression as he eyed Kindred and casually thrust his hands deep in the pockets of his coat. "I don't understand," he said. "Cathy must know what's in back of it."

"Suppose you tell us what is."

The curt quality to Kindred's words roused an obvious anger in Codrick. "Us?" he bridled. "You mean I have to include you in something that's not even slightly your affair?"

"Yes, Hugh. You do."

Cathy's words took Kindred unawares. But if they surprised him, they surprised the lawyer even more. For the first time a definite uncertainty edged into Codrick's glance. "This isn't like you, Cathy," he said in an injured tone. "Am I being cross-examined?"

Kindred suddenly decided to put an end to this verbal fencing. He could think of only one way of doing it. He said bluntly, "Codrick, I've seen Martin Semple tonight."

The fleeting alarm that brightened the look in the lawyer's eyes was unmistakable. He asked haltingly, "Should that mean something to me?"

"We know about the Difficult," came Kindred's brittle words. "We know how you made him lie to Grace."

Codrick looked quickly at the girl. "Cathy, this is . . . I don't even begin to know what he's —"

"We know a few more things," Kindred cut in on him. "You hired Reno to watch Grace. You had him turn the sheep out last night, didn't you? He had to be the one who shot Noah. That was probably an accident. Then tonight when you found out he was in jail you decided he might talk and tell what he knew about you. You went up there and killed him. You —"

Kindred saw the lawyer's right hand move against the heavy fur of the coat. He knew at once that his fury had dulled his wariness, that Codrick had a gun in his pocket. And just as surely he understood that there was no time to reach to the Colt at his waist.

The next split-second his instinct made him push Cathy aside and wheel hard away from her. He had the time to breathe a gusty sigh of thankfulness at seeing Codrick's body swing with his move, out of line with Cathy. Then with a powerful shove of his left arm he swept the stack of trays from the counter, throwing them straight at Codrick, lunging at the man.

The lawyer jerked to one side as the trays whirled toward him. The flat explosion of the gun in his pocket filled the room with deafening sound. Kindred felt the pound of a blow along his left thigh as the trays clattered to the floor. His leg all at once gave way under him. He fell crookedly, taking a last awkward stride in on Codrick.

He reached out as he fell and caught a tight hold on the lawyer's coat. Codrick was jerking the gun clear as Kindred hauled him off his feet. He swung the Colt club-fashion as he went down, swung it at Kindred's face, and the weapon's sight laid open a long gash the length of Kindred's cheek.

Codrick was frantic now and struck out with the gun once more, and missed. He clawed his way free of Kindred's hold and lunged erect. But then a swing of Kindred's good leg caught him hard against the shins, and he cried out in fear and pain, trying to wheel away.

Kindred thought again of his gun. But he lay with his right arm pinned under him. He pushed himself up with that arm and made an awkward, sprawling dive at the man's legs as Codrick tried to aim the Colt once more. Kindred heard Cathy scream a split-second before the gun's blast rattled the windows. He felt the bullet sear the top of the thick muscle along his right shoulder. Then his arms were sweeping the lawyer's legs from under him.

Codrick fell with a force that shook the floor. And as he lay momentarily stunned, Kindred pulled his right arm free and rolled onto his side to reach for his gun. Codrick saw this and in panic kicked out wickedly with both feet. One boot-heel struck Kindred a numbing blow on the right arm. And during the second it took Kindred to move against the pain, the lawyer rolled onto his feet and lunged wildly for the door.

He was staring back at Kindred, his eyes wide in crazed fear as he moved. He saw the swift, sure way Kindred's hand brushed his coat aside and lifted the .45 out. He realized then that he couldn't reach the door. He wheeled, jerking the Colt up.

His move was too violent, too hurried, and the shot he threw shattered the glass front of the counter a foot above the line of Kindred's outstretched shape. He made a frantic effort to thumb back the hammer of the Colt again. Then the gun exploded up at him.

A look of outright amazement crossed his handsome face. He staggered backward toward the window, the Colt falling from his suddenly weakened grip. The window sill all at once caught him at the back of the knees. He doubled over, trying vainly to catch his balance. Then he tottered outward, making an ungainly futile reach for the window's edge.

The glass all at once gave way against his weight, jangling dissonantly into the snow that billowed up to swallow his falling, crippled shape.

It was over. That certainty all at once dawned on Kindred as he rested the hand that held the gun against the floor. For the first time he was feeling the deep ache in his thigh, the burning at his shoulder. But then he forgot that as he heard the rustle of Cathy's dress behind him and turned his head to look up at her.

Her tear-filled eyes were bright with thankfulness and adoration as she knelt close beside him. Very gently, she reached up and touched his gashed cheek. Then, with a look he was never to forget, she put her lips to his.

Grace Hill hurried in off the street some twenty minutes after two men had helped Kindred on back to Cathy's room and others from the crowd that gathered on the walk had carried Codrick's body away. Grace found Pete Ballew, Fred Ordway and another man rigging a canvas across the broken window, and at once asked Ordway, "Where is he, Fred?"

Ordway nodded to the rear of the building. Before he had the chance to speak she queried hesitantly, "Is it as bad as they say?"

"Could've been a lot worse," he told her. "He'll have to favor that leg for awhile is all."

"Thank heaven," she breathed. "Can I see him?"

"Go right ahead."

Cathy answered Grace's knock on the rear room's door. The girl smiled when she saw who it was and stepped wordlessly aside so that Grace could look on into the room.

Kindred sat in a chair by the stove, his back half turned. He looked around to see who it was. And sight of the livid gash along his swollen cheek made Grace catch her breath. Nevertheless, she showed none of her qualms as she came into the room and stood in front of him. Her glance took in the sling on his arm, the bulge of bandage at his thigh and the dark smear around the tear in the cloth of his trousers.

Then she was smiling broadly in answer to the crooked semblance of a grin he gave her. "The Lord looks after fools and children. Jeff, I got you into this, didn't I?"

"You helped," he admitted. "The way it turned out, it was a good thing you did."

"Yes. But it might've turned out another way." Grace sighed. But then, noticing that

Cathy had put her arm across the back of Kindred's chair, the severity of her expression eased before a shrewd, knowing look. In another moment she glanced down at Kindred to say, "Something's happened to you two."

The color in his face deepened. It was Cathy who quietly told her, "Something has, Grace."

The old woman's smile came once more, broader than it had been. "Now isn't that the queerest thing. I knew it this evening when I was talking to you, Cathy. Just as sure as I knew Hugh Codrick was in for a surprise. It was Jeff this, Jeff that."

She saw the look of confusion on both their faces and laughed softly, afterward saying in all seriousness, "Nothing's ever pleased me so much."

Kindred and Cathy had nothing to say, and shortly Grace was telling them, "I've had a talk with Martin Semple. He told me everything, or at least all he knew. Jeff, he asked me to say he wanted to see you but was afraid to. I'm sorry as can be for that man."

Glancing up at Cathy, Kindred drawled, "This about Semple goes no further than the three of us. I gave him my word tonight no one would ever find out what he did, which is why I pretended not to know him when you mentioned his name."

Cathy nodded. Then Grace was saying, "Now's no time for me to ask what all happened. But you can tell me one thing. The man that was killed at the jail was the same man who'd been watching me up at the mine, wasn't he?"

"The same," Kindred answered. "Reno. Codrick killed him."

"So I heard out on the street. Codrick must have been brother of the devil." Grace's glance took on a quality of tenderness then as she regarded Kindred and abruptly announced, "Jeff, Martin says my hunch was right about the Difficult. I've made the strike Mr. Hill always dreamed of. So sometime soon now you and Cathy will be having lease money. A lot of it."

She took in their surprise and, seeing that Kindred was almost to speak, said quickly, "Martin Semple's writing a mining man, asking him to come in and look over what I've found. He says this man will want to bring in machinery and a crew to open up the Difficult again. Which means we'll have to draw up a new lease."

"A new one?" Kindred's look was faintly troubled. "Why?"

"Because I'm old and a woman. Because

he's going to take a man to manage things up there. You're to be the man, Jeff. And you're going to collect a far bigger share than this present lease gives Ladder."

"But I don't want more," Kindred protested, wincing as he rose awkwardly from the chair.

He saw her step to the door now and open it and said sharply, "Wait now, Grace!"

She looked around, giving him a smile, saying, "There's nothing you can do about it, Jeff. This is the way I want it." Then, nodding, she said, "Good night, you two," as she stepped out and closed the door.

Kindred faced around, staring helplessly at Cathy. "She can't do this, Catherine. This is something she's worked years for. I won't see her give it away."

"If I know Grace, she'll do exactly as she pleases."

She reached up and ran a hand lightly over his dark head, the expression in her eyes making him put everything from mind but her closeness. He took her in his arms, thinking of his tomorrows then, of how full and rich this night had made their promise.

**Peter Dawson** is the *nom de plume* used by Jonathan Hurff Glidden for all of his fiction. It was also used once by Frederick Faust, better known as Max Brand, for a magazine story, and by Otis Gaylord for a series of eight novels. The name itself is derived from a popular brand of Scotch whiskey. Glidden was born in Kewanee, Illinois, and was graduated from the University of Illinois with a degree in English literature. He came first to write Western fiction because of prompting from his brother Frederick Dilley Glidden who wrote Western fiction under the pseudonym Luke Short. In his career as a Western writer, he has written sixteen Western novels and over 120 Western novelettes and short stories for the magazine market. Glidden from the beginning was a dedicated craftsman who revised and polished his fiction until it shone as a fine gem. His Peter Dawson novels are noted for their adept plotting, interesting and well developed characters, their authentically researched historical backgrounds, and his stylistic flair. His first novel THE CRIMSON HORSESHOE won the Dodd, Mead Prize as the best Western of the year 1941 and ran serially in Street and Smith's WESTERN STORY MAGAZINE prior to book publication. During the

Second World War, Glidden served with the U.S. Strategic and Tactical Air Force in the United Kingdom. Later in 1950 he served for a time as Assistant to Chief of Station in Germany. After the war, his novels were frequently serialized in THE SATURDAY EVENING POST. In paperback, his books have already sold 25,000,000 copies worldwide and have been translated into numerous foreign languages. Dawson titles such as HIGH COUNTRY, GUNSMOKE GRAZE, and ROYAL GORGE are generally conceded to be among his masterpieces although he was an extremely consistent writer and virtually all his fiction has retained its classic stature among readers of all generations. His short story "Long Gone" (1950) was adapted for the screen as FACE OF A FUGITIVE (Columbia, 1959) starring Fred MacMurray and James Coburn. His earlier classic Western novels are being reprinted in hardcover by Chivers, Ltd., for the English-reading world and many of his longer novel-length titles, beginning with RATTLESNAKE MESA, are appearing for the first time in book form.

We hope you have enjoyed this Large Print book. Other Thorndike Press or Chivers Press Large Print books are available at your library or directly from the publishers.

For more information about current and upcoming titles, please call or write, without obligation, to:

Thorndike Press
P.O. Box 159
Thorndike, Maine 04986 USA
Tel. (800) 223-2336

OR

Chivers Press Limited
Windsor Bridge Road
Bath BA2 3AX
England
Tel. (0225) 335336

All our Large Print titles are designed for easy reading, and all our books are made to last.

143